Dominion

The Ultimatum

Boundaries

To Love and Submit
To Love and Trust
To Love and Obey

Anthologies

Over the Knee

Single Titles

Kneel for You

TO LOVE AND SUBMIT

KATY SWANN

Dedication

Thank you to my ever-patient and loving family for all your support.

Chapter One

Rachel moaned indulgently as the man slid easily into her deliciously wet pussy. He was big, so very big, and as he filled her with his long, thick shaft, she wondered briefly if she could take the full length of him as he pushed himself farther into her. Just when she thought she would burst, though, he pulled slowly out and a slight hint of a smile appeared in his eyes as they commanded her to surrender to him completely. Desperate to feel him inside her again, she tried to pull him back, begging him with her eyes to take her. Just as she raised her hips urgently toward him, he plunged deeply back into her, filling her completely and making her cry out with pleasure.

"Good girl," he growled, "let me hear you scream."

"Yes, Sir," she cried, knowing he would be expecting her to respond and, as she did so, he rewarded her with a harder, deeper thrust. She wanted to touch him so badly, to run her fingers along his perfect, muscular body and, in a desperate attempt to get closer to him, she tugged at the cuffs that bound her wrists to the rail at the head of the bed. She soon forgot about them, though, as she felt a sharp slap on the side of her thigh and the desperate need in her intensified as her body responded with a delicious shudder.

"Again?" His voice was rich and deep, and behind the hard line of his lips lurked a smile that promised more delights to come.

"Yes please, Sir," she whispered, her voice now hoarse with emotion and lust.

"Pardon? I didn't hear you." Another slap and her body quivered uncontrollably in response to the hot sting his hand left on her buttock.

"Yes, yes, yes..." she cried. But then, devastating reality began to force its way into her consciousness as she slowly woke from her dream. *"Yes... Oh, shit!"*

She sat up in her bed, painfully alone and very aroused. Shit, it had felt so real, his voice, his body, everything. She rubbed her wrists, fully expecting the marks from the cuffs to be visible but, of course, there were no marks, no cuffs and no gorgeous man demanding her compliance.

Rachel sighed, resigned once more to gratification thanks to her trusted and reliable Rabbit. As she reached under her bed, she tried to conjure up the image of the strong lover who had just been ravishing her in her dream. This was the fifth time she had had this dream, always with the same man, and yet she could never recall his face once she woke. No matter how hard she tried, he remained an elusive fantasy only willing to appear in her sleep.

She moved her hand down under her duvet and quickly checked that she was nice and wet for her battery operated lover. Yep, she was definitely ready and she quickly slipped the cold, hard device into her wetness then flicked the switch. Nothing happened. She pulled it out again and fumbled with the various settings, but still it remained stubbornly silent and still.

Shit, shit and double shit, the fucking batteries were dead. This was not a good start to the day, she thought, as she reached down to finish with her fingers.

Half an hour later, she stomped into the kitchen, now showered and dressed, and grunted a half-hearted greeting at her flatmate, Mandy.

"What's the matter with you?" asked her friend with a smirk. "From what I heard, you should be grinning like a Cheshire Cat."

Rachel stared at Mandy in shock. "What?"

"Sweetie, the walls are very thin in this flat, in case you didn't know. Either you've got a secret lover hidden away in that room of yours, or you've been playing with your bunny again." Mandy winked at her and handed her a cup of fresh coffee.

Rachel sighed. "I had that dream again, you know, the

one where this gorgeous man straps me to the bed and has his wicked way with me? Well, it's getting more intense." She took a sip of her coffee and felt a shiver run through her body as she remembered the feel of the cuffs holding her arms above her head. It had felt so incredibly sexy, and yet she wasn't normally into kinky stuff like that, so it didn't make sense that she'd be having such erotic dreams about it. The trouble was, now that the idea was so firmly planted in her head, she couldn't stop thinking about it and the more she thought about it, the more the idea of being tethered to a bed and at the complete mercy of a strong, dominant man excited her.

Mandy stuck some bread in the toaster and came to sit next to Rachel at the small kitchen table. "What you need, my friend, is a man. One who's into the same kinky sex as you."

"I'm not into kinky sex. Just because I've had a few weird dreams about being tied up doesn't turn me into a bloody Dominatrix."

"Of course not," Mandy looked at Rachel as if she was stupid. "A Dominatrix is the one who does the tying up. You like to be tied up, which makes you the submissive."

Rachel nearly choked on her coffee. "I am *not* a submissive. I've never been tied up in my life for God's sake!"

"Except in your dreams." Mandy got up to retrieve the hot toast as it popped up. "All I'm saying is, you've obviously got this hot fantasy and there's no smoke without fire and all that shit. Toast?"

Rachel took a slice of the slightly blackened toast and stared at it absently. "Yeah, but the way I'm going I'll never meet anyone and, even if I did, they'd probably run a mile if I hinted that I might want to experiment with a bit of bondage."

Mandy chuckled. "I wouldn't count on it. Most single, straight men would jump at the chance of tying up a gorgeous woman and fucking her senseless."

Rachel laughed at her friend's rather crude but probably

accurate statement. "Well, I don't know any single, straight men, except for Mike Jones at work." Mike was the Facilities Manager who had been harboring a crush on her for months. He was very sweet, but middle-aged, overweight and had a serious BO problem.

Mandy's eyebrows shot up. "You have got to be joking! Okay, babe, we've got to get you sorted before you end up shagging the likes of Mike Jones."

"Yes, but how? There's no way I'm going to some seedy club to pick up a complete stranger." Taking a bite of the toast, Rachel shrugged. "Even if I was that desperate I wouldn't want the risk of picking up some nutter."

Mandy studied her for a second and sighed. "You know, you could join an Internet dating site. I'd bet there are a few that cater for people into BDSM and stuff."

"No way, I'm definitely not that desperate, and anyway, I don't really know if I am into all that stuff. I don't want to lead some scary dominant man on, only to find that it's not what I want after all."

"Rachel, Internet dating sites are perfectly okay, you know. You don't have to be desperate or weird to join one — loads of normal, attractive people sign up, and if you just express a mild interest in BDSM, you're not committing yourself to a fully fledged Dom."

Rachel sighed as she finished her toast. Maybe Mandy had a point. It wouldn't hurt to search for a few sites when she got a spare moment at work. Their own computer had crashed a couple of days ago and seemed to have given up the ghost, so the only Internet connection she had access to for now was the one at work, although it was strictly forbidden to use it for personal stuff.

"I'll think about it." She smiled at Mandy, wishing she was more like her. Whereas she was petite and skinny, Mandy was tall and statuesque with gorgeous tanned skin and brown eyes, compared to her own pasty pale complexion and green eyes. Whether it was her height and striking cheekbones that gave Mandy so much confidence,

Rachel didn't know, but she envied her flatmate's ability to make friends so easily and the way she had men falling over themselves to go out with her.

Mandy reached out, took Rachel's hand and gave it a squeeze. "Hey, I'm really glad you're thinking about sex again. It's been over a year since you and Paul broke up, so it's about time."

"Mandy..." At the mention of Paul, Rachel stood up and dumped her plate and mug in the sink. She hated talking about him so that meant the end of that particular conversation as far as she was concerned.

"Okay, I know, I mustn't talk about *him*. Anyway, I'm off. See you tonight." Mandy blew her a quick kiss and grabbed her bag.

"Yeah, bye."

Rachel didn't move for at least ten minutes after Mandy left. Her mind was racing with thoughts about this online dating stuff. The idea of meeting some gorgeous hunk who would introduce her to a new world of erotic play, maybe tie her up—spank her even—sent a shudder of excitement through her entire body.

She sighed as memories of Paul returned to haunt her. Would she ever get over him? Mandy was right, it was more than a year since he'd so cruelly dumped her, with tragic consequences, and yet the pain was still as strong as it had been then. Well, there was no way she would ever let a man get to her like that again. If she did meet someone through one of these sites, it would be strictly sex only. Love was seriously off the menu, and until now that had meant sex was as well, but, as her dreams were so persistently reminding her, maybe it was time to give her body a little treat.

Forty minutes later, Rachel tiptoed past her boss's office in the vain hope that he wouldn't notice she was ten minutes late. She had been so preoccupied on the Tube that she'd missed her stop and had had to walk back to Holborn, stopping at Starbucks on the way of course. She carefully put her coffee cup on her desk and slid into her chair, silently congratulating herself for not getting caught, when she heard Joe call, "Rachel!"

Damn, he sounded angry. As she scurried toward his office door, she wondered why he was so rattled about her being a teeny bit late. He wasn't normally so anal about her timekeeping.

"Hi, Joe," she called brightly, as she burst through the door. One look at his face confirmed her fears – something was definitely wrong. His normally calm composure was gone – instead he looked like he might want to kill her. She tried to recall what had happened yesterday and was just about to reassure herself that she hadn't made any personal calls or done anything she shouldn't have, when she remembered the search on her computer.

She'd only wanted to check one tiny little thing, something that had been bugging her for a while that she couldn't wait to know the answer to. Oh God, she'd done a search on BDSM and what the letters stood for and Joe must have found out. She'd known what the S and M stood for and guessed that the B must have been for bondage, but she hadn't been sure about the D. She had felt a delicious warmth spread through her body as she'd read the description of discipline and dominance, but she hadn't had time to finish reading it all so she'd bookmarked the page intending to finish it later. Shit, how was she going to explain that one? She put on her best 'I don't know what you're talking about' smile and said, "Anything wrong?"

"Yes, Rachel, very fucking wrong." Joe stood up and started pacing the small office, his red, round face glowing with rage.

"I was only checking for a friend..." she stammered.

"Fucking Adam Stone," he interrupted before she could finish. "He may be the CEO of this company, but what gives him the right to steal other people's staff?" He stopped suddenly and gave her a hard stare. "Checking what?"

"Oh, nothing. Train times." She could feel her face flush,

but he was too angry to notice.

"Come and sit down," he said, with a sharp edge to his voice.

She was seriously worried now. She had never seen her normally placid boss so agitated. She quickly sat down without another word and waited for him to tell her what was going on.

He returned to his chair and sat down opposite, glaring at her before his eyes softened slightly. "I'm sorry, Rachel, it's not your fault. I'm just so bloody angry, you know?"

No, she didn't know, he hadn't actually told her anything yet. "Joe? What's happened? Why are you so mad?" Her voice was gentle. She liked Joe and hated seeing him this upset.

He sighed, as if finally resigning himself to the fact that there was nothing he could do. "Adam Stone's PA is pregnant," he stated, simply.

That was it? What did Lucy being pregnant have to do with Joe? Oh no, surely not... "Rachel Porter, I can read you like a book. No, I did not get Lucy pregnant!" Despite his anger, his lips curled up into a reluctant smile and he visibly relaxed a bit.

"Why is Lucy's pregnancy such a problem for you?" she asked, frowning.

"Because there have been complications and she's been ordered bed rest for the duration of the pregnancy, with immediate effect." He was staring at her as if that would explain his outburst, but of course it didn't. Then the bombshell fell. "Stone wants you to replace her."

Rachel's jaw dropped. "What? Me? Why?"

"Stone hates temps, refuses to work with them. He has a policy that if Lucy is ever off work, one of the other senior PAs fills in and their boss gets the temp. But Brenda is on sick leave and Hilary leaves at the end of the week." Joe glared at Rachel with resentment as he spat out his next words, "You're next in line."

"But... Joe, I don't want to work for Mr Stone." The truth

was, Adam Stone scared her shitless. He had a reputation for being ruthless and had reduced many a PA to tears. In fact, she was close to tears herself right now.

Joe smiled at her, not a warm, reassuring smile, but a bitter, defeated one that told her it was no use trying to make him change his mind. It wasn't his decision to make. "I'm sorry, Rachel, but the boss has spoken and the rest of us have no choice but to toe the line. You're to make your way up to his office immediately and I wouldn't take too long about it. Stone is not a man who likes to be kept waiting."

Rachel felt tears sting her eyes. This was turning out to be one hell of a shitty day and she had a really bad feeling that it was about to get a hell of a lot worse.

Chapter Two

As Rachel stepped into the executive lift that would take her to the top floor, she felt her legs grow weak with nerves. She wasn't the right person for this job. She was just a secretary who happened to have worked for the same boss for over six years. It was a comfortable and unchallenging role, made even better because she got on well with Joe, her easy-going and undemanding boss.

It was well known that Adam Stone demanded perfection, in every aspect. Lucy, his present PA, was a stylish graduate whose cool efficiency had the respect of every employee at Stone Media. How the hell was she going to fill shoes like that?

She couldn't do shorthand and her organizational skills left a lot to be desired. Last month she had accidently booked Joe onto a flight to Geneva when he was meant to have been heading to Genoa for a big conference. She had been blissfully unaware of her huge blunder until she'd gotten a furious call from Joe, who had been stuck at Heathrow watching the Genoa flight take off without him. God, he'd been mad, but she had just about managed to save her skin by getting him on the last Genoa flight out of London, which he'd made with about a minute to spare.

Well, Genoa/Geneva—they sounded almost the same—surely anyone would have made that mistake? Well, maybe not, which was why she wasn't the right person to do this job. Joe had eventually forgiven her—just—but imagine if she did that to Adam Stone? Her stomach clenched into a tight knot just thinking about it.

The lift came to a stop with a little ping and the doors

opened, exposing the lush reception area of the sleek top floor. She hesitated briefly before stepping tentatively out into the line of fire.

"Oh, there you are," Hilary, the Finance Director's PA, snapped at her. "Come on, I'll show you to your office. Mr Stone is out so you'll have a few minutes to orientate yourself. I'll be around till the end of the week if you need anything, but then I leave and you'll be on your own. You'll have to show my replacement the ropes as you'll be the most senior PA so you'd better get to grips with the work quickly." Her tone was brisk and efficient, a bit like her polished, businesslike appearance. She stopped at a glass fronted office and gestured for Rachel to go through the open door.

"This is your office. The password to Lucy's computer is written in a notebook in the top drawer of the desk and the kitchen for tea and coffee is opposite the lifts." With that, she walked off, leaving Rachel staring after her like an abandoned puppy. She wanted to run after her and beg her not to leave her alone, but Hilary clearly had her own boss to get back to. Besides which, she didn't want to appear completely useless in front of her new, and less than friendly, colleague.

So she remained where she was, alone in the silent office, glancing helplessly around. The carpet was a deep blue color, plush and very expensive by the looks of it, and she felt it squish under her feet as she crossed toward a large mahogany desk by the back wall. A couple of pictures of Mr Stone meeting important people hung on the perfectly painted white walls and she stopped and studied them closely. He was a formidable man, not only in reputation, but in appearance as well. He easily towered over the other men in the pictures and the cold blue eyes that glared into the camera commanded uncompromising respect. She'd met him a couple of times at corporate parties, and, despite his cold and tough demeanor, she'd had a bit of a crush on him as she'd watched him from afar.

14

She turned away from the pictures to face her new desk and felt a wave of despair. How the hell had she ended up in this position? *I don't want to be here*, she cried silently. It took all her strength not to run back downstairs and hide behind Joe's desk. Now, there was a thought—maybe she could convince Joe to refuse to let her go. Surely he had some say in this? But the memory of his defeated face told her that he hadn't wanted her to go any more than she had, and she knew it would be pointless trying.

Suddenly, the phone shrilled, shattering the silence and dragging Rachel's mind out of Joe's office and back to her new one. After an initial moment of panic, she rushed forward and grabbed the receiver before it could divert back to reception. "Mr Stone's office, can I help you?" she said, as efficiently as she could.

"Lucy?"

"Er, no, Lucy is on leave, this is Rachel Porter."

Rachel heard an exasperated sigh on the other end of the line. "Oh. This is Linda, Lord Granville's PA. Are you Lucy's replacement?" The voice sounded impatient and ultra-confident, and Rachel tried to echo Linda's tone in her reply.

"Yes, that's right. How can I help you?"

"Lord Granville needs to see Mr Stone today at three o'clock. Is he available?" Linda's curt tone gave the impression that a negative answer was not an option. But Rachel wasn't even logged on to her computer yet so she couldn't access Mr Stone's diary. *Oh, dear, not a good start*, she thought with a sinking feeling.

"I'm sorry, Linda, I can't give you an answer right now as there's a problem with the computer system. IT are looking at it as we speak, so can I call you back in a few minutes?" She bloody well wasn't going to admit that she didn't even know how to access Mr Stone's diary yet, and at least this would give her a few minutes to acquaint herself with Lucy's computer before she called Linda back.

"Hmm," came the disgruntled reply. "Don't take too

long, Lord Granville needs an answer." And with that, the phone went dead before Rachel had a chance to ask for her number.

Rachel replaced the receiver and rummaged in the drawer for Lucy's notebook. *I'll show them I can be just as good as Linda, Miss Snooty PA of the Year*, she thought with new-found determination. In which case, it might be a good idea to get her bearings before Mr Stone came back as right then she didn't know Mr Stone's office from the stationery cupboard. There was a door in the frosted glass wall to her right and she guessed that would most likely be Mr Stone's office so she headed there first. As she poked her head round the door she let out a small gasp.

Adam Stone's office was beautiful – large, airy and very stylish. The office was situated at the corner of the building, giving the room two walls of glass looking out onto the London skyline. In the corner, where the windows met, stood an enormous mahogany desk, similar to hers – only much bigger and completely clutter-free. In the other corner was a suite of black leather sofas and chairs neatly placed around a glass coffee table. To the left of them was an open door leading into a small private meeting room and next to that was Mr Stone's private bathroom suite.

Wow, how the other half live, she thought, as she made her way across the office to look out at the view. And it really was exceptional – Big Ben towered proudly over the horizon, competing for dominance with the many grandiose spires and towers, and in the far distance she could just about make out the top of the London Eye.

Without realizing it, Rachel lost track of time as she became mesmerized by the sight in front of her.

"Enjoying the view?"

Rachel's stomach jumped at the same time as her body and she swung round quickly to find herself face to face with Adam Stone. His tall frame filled the doorway as he stood with his arms crossed, watching her with a bemused look on his face.

"I...er... I was just..." Rachel felt a rush of heat shoot up from her neck to her face. Oh crap, she seemed to have lost the power of speech as she squirmed under his intense gaze.

"Enjoying the view, yes, I think we've established that. I take it you're Miss Porter?" His smooth, deep voice held a hint of humor as he watched her struggling to compose herself.

"Yes, Mr Stone. I'm Rachel Porter." She wiped her clammy palms on her skirt as she watched him cross his office and sit down in the large leather chair behind his desk. A vague memory suddenly sprang to mind about him having been a semi-pro football player when he was younger. She could easily imagine that because under his crisply ironed white shirt she could see tight muscles stretch across his broad chest and shoulders. She was aware of her pulse quickening slightly as she wondered what he would look like without that shirt...

"Still enjoying the view, Miss Porter?" Mr Stone's deep voice snapped Rachel out of her erotic reverie and she quickly recovered her air of professional detachment before he could notice the blush threatening to burn her cheeks again.

"I was just going to ask if I could get you a coffee," she said, coolly. She was damned if she was going to let him see her get all flustered, so she held his gaze and waited expectantly for his answer.

Adam Stone sat back in his chair and a smile played subtly on his lips. "Yes, thank you."

"Okay, coming right up," she said, efficiently, and turned to leave, but then she stopped again and turned back to Mr Stone. "Er, sorry. How do you take it?"

Adam Stone's eyebrows rose in amusement and his sharp blue eyes held hers as he said, "How do I take what, Miss Porter?"

"Er...your coffee." Rachel could feel her face flush again and prayed that he didn't notice.

Luckily he was now studying his iPhone as he mumbled,

"Black, no sugar." She was clearly dismissed so she scurried out to the small kitchen as quickly as she could, relieved to get away.

She closed the kitchen door behind her and leaned back against it, closing her eyes as she relived her first encounter with Adam Stone. Wow, the guy was intense. Intense, powerful and gorgeous—a lethal combination as far as she was concerned. Well, she wasn't going to let the fact that he was so hot affect the way she would do her job. No way!

A few minutes later, she marched back into Mr Stone's office with a renewed air of confidence and placed his coffee down in front of him.

"Not there!" he snapped. "Use the coaster, this desk is solid mahogany." He glared angrily at her and nodded his head to a discreet stack of coasters on the shelf beside the desk. Rachel tried her best to keep her hand steady as she picked up a coaster and placed the hot porcelain mug carefully onto it, but it wouldn't stop shaking and she came perilously close to spilling coffee all over the expensive desk.

"Sit down," he commanded without looking up from his phone. She did as she'd been told and waited for him to finish reading. She crossed her legs and stole a quick look at him across the desk. Although he had the ruggedness of a football player, along with a slightly crooked nose, he really was extremely good-looking. His dark hair was streaked with shades of silver giving him an elegant, distinguished look and his strong jaw reminded her a bit of a 1950s film star.

Suddenly he looked up from the phone and smiled. Rachel flushed as she realized he had two dimples in his cheeks that instantly upgraded him from merely good-looking to drop dead gorgeous. "Sorry about that, Miss Porter. Now, have you been fully briefed on what's required of you?"

"Er... Yes, thank you, Mr Stone," she stammered. *If you can call Hilary's curt introduction a briefing*, she thought, grudgingly, but didn't voice it.

"Good. If you have any questions, Hilary is just down the corridor." He studied her for a moment, his sharp blue eyes running slowly over her upper body. To her dismay, Rachel felt her nipples harden under his gaze. She couldn't tell if he noticed or not, but he looked calmly back at her flushed face and said, "I expect you to be immaculately turned out at all times, business suits, hair tied up, not too much makeup."

"Er, okay." She realized she probably wasn't looking her best today after her rather frustrating morning. She'd just grabbed the first blouse she could find, which badly needed ironing, and her long blonde hair hung loosely around her shoulders—she certainly didn't look like someone who was smart enough to be Adam Stone's PA. Damn, of all the days she hadn't made an effort, she had to pick today.

"Yes, *Sir*." Mr Stone's voice cut through her thoughts.

"Pardon?"

"You will address me as Sir."

Shit, is he for real? Rachel felt her face redden even more as she struggled to control her temper. Who did he think he was? Suddenly his handsome face didn't look quite so appealing as he coldly asserted his authority over her. But, instead of showing her annoyance, she just looked meekly back at him and nodded.

"Yes, Sir," she said, through gritted teeth.

"Good. Now, there are a couple of things I need to go through with you before I head off to my next meeting." But as he opened his desk drawer and took out some papers, his mobile phone rang. He quickly checked the caller display.

"Excuse me," he said, before answering the call.

"George! How are you?" He swung his chair around to face the window and, once he had his back to her, she took a deep breath. *Oh God, I'm not going to be able to do this.* She glared at the back of Mr Stone's head, suddenly hating him for making her feel so inadequate. She was on the verge of standing up and walking out when pride made her remain firmly seated. If she ran away from this job, she'd never be able to face her colleagues, or herself, for that matter, again. She needed this job and she would bloody well show *Sir* fucking Adam Stone that she could do it. Straightening herself in the chair, she lifted her head and resolved not to give in.

But just as she did so, Mr Stone swung back around in his chair and narrowed his eyes at her. "Did she, now?" he asked, coldly.

Oh no, what I have done? Rachel had no doubt that he was talking about her, but it was only half past nine in the morning so surely she couldn't have screwed up already, could she? Mr Stone ended the call and gave her an angry glare, confirming her fears.

"Did you get a phone call from George Granville's PA this morning?" His voice was controlled and steady, but it sounded deadly nonetheless.

Oh fuck! A cold chill crept through Rachel as she remembered Miss Snooty PA's words earlier. She was meant to call her straight back, but she'd gone exploring around the office instead and Mr Stone had returned. *Oh, no.*

"I...er..."

"Answer me!" Mr Stone raised his voice and Rachel felt tears well up in her eyes as he crossed his arms and waited for her explanation.

"Yes, Sir, I did. I had only just arrived in the office and hadn't yet managed to access the online diary and then... I forgot." Her voice trailed off as she realized how pathetic she sounded.

"For God's sake, have you any idea how bad this looks to Lord Granville?" he snapped.

"I'm really sorry, it won't happen again." The tears were threatening to spill and Rachel tried desperately to hold onto her composure as any remaining pride was replaced with shame.

"Too right, it won't," he growled. "Get back to your desk before I fire you on the spot."

"Yes, Sir. I'm sorry." Rachel scrambled out of the chair and headed quickly for the door of Mr Stone's office, but just as she approached it, she heard him mutter, "Under different circumstances, I'd put you over my fucking knee."

Rachel ran out of his office, back to the relative safety of her desk before she fully acknowledged his words. Shit, did he just say he'd put her over his knee? Disbelief, mingled with something that felt shockingly like arousal, washed over her and it took a few minutes before she was able to compose herself enough to log on to Lucy's computer and focus her mind back on work.

Chapter Three

"I hate Adam Fucking Stone!" Rachel slammed the door to the flat shut and threw her bag onto the floor, frustration and anger coming together and surging through her body in another wave of despair.

Almost immediately, Mandy's head popped around her bedroom door. "What's up with you?" she asked, frowning.

"You wouldn't believe the day I've had." Rachel, who was normally so calm and even-tempered, kicked her bag roughly out of the way and marched into the kitchen. "Have we got any wine?"

"Yes, there's a bottle of red in the top cupboard. Give me two minutes and I'll join you," Mandy called back from her room.

Rachel found the wine, but groaned in annoyance when she saw it was topped with a cork. "Who the hell buys wine that doesn't have a screw top?" she grumbled, as she rummaged through a drawer looking for the corkscrew.

Her day really had gone from bad to worse. Adam Stone was a demanding bastard, constantly snapping or shouting at her. She had barely had time to log on to her computer when he'd told her to bring her notepad into his office, which she'd done with a strained smile on her face, only to find that he wanted her to take some dictation.

He hadn't been too impressed when she'd told him she didn't know shorthand. To make matters worse, when Lord Granville had turned up for the three o'clock meeting, Mr Stone had reprimanded her in front of him and had forced her to apologize profusely, making her feel like a naughty schoolgirl. She had come *that* close to telling him where to stick his bloody job. It had only been pride that she wouldn't show him any weakness that had stopped her, but what about tomorrow, and the day after that, when there was no pride left?

"So what's wrong, then?" Mandy walked into the kitchen and took the wine from Rachel's trembling hands. "Here, let me do that before you break the cork."

"Oh, Mandy, I've had the shittiest day ever. I'm never going back there, that arsehole will have to find someone else to pick on." A sob broke from her and she quickly grabbed the glass Mandy was holding out to her and took a big gulp.

Mandy took her arm and led her through to the living room. "Come on, babe, tell me what happened."

Rachel told Mandy everything, from Joe's unwelcome news when she had arrived that morning, to her big fuck-up with Lord Granville. "The thing is, Mandy, I'm only a secretary, not a PA. That's why I work for Joe on half the salary that Lucy's on, but Mr Stone didn't seem to take that into consideration. He treated me like I was some sort of idiot. I *hate* him."

"Oh, sweetie, you've got to stick with it. After all, it's not permanent, is it? How long before Lucy's replacement was due to start?" When Rachel looked at her blankly, she added, "Lucy would have gone on maternity leave just before the baby was due so Mr Stone would have had to have a replacement by then, wouldn't he? You were never meant to cover her actual maternity leave so he must have someone else lined up."

"Yeah, I suppose." The reminder that this probably wouldn't be a permanent situation made Rachel feel a little bit better. If she could only grit her teeth and keep her head down until the maternity cover started, she could go back to working for Joe and everything would return to normal.

Mandy gently prodded Rachel's arm. "Here's something to cheer you up. My normally useless big brother came by today and has fixed the computer—we're connected with the outside world again so let's go find some dating sites."

Rachel frowned. After the day she'd had, that was the last thing she felt like doing. "Can we do it tomorrow? I'm really not in the mood," she groaned, taking another large swig of wine.

"Oh, come on, grumpy, it'll help you forget about work. Get your arse over here and help me do a search."

With a sigh of resignation, Rachel dragged herself off the sofa and joined Mandy at the computer desk, an old wooden gardening table they had salvaged in a junk shop and painted bright pink. Pulling up a chair, she watched Mandy log on and wished she felt a bit more enthusiastic.

"Right, let's save a bit of time here." Mandy grinned as the search page awaited their instructions. "You're especially interested in meeting someone who's into BDSM, right?"

"Yeah, I suppose." Rachel downed the rest of the wine in her glass and automatically reached over to pour herself another.

"Steady on, girl, you've got to work tomorrow, remember?"

"How could I forget?" Rachel scowled, taking another large swig.

"Okay, here goes. Let's start by Googling BDSM Internet social sites and see what comes up." As Mandy hit the return key, page after page of results showed up and she let out a little squeal of delight. "Ooh look, Rach, there are loads of them."

Despite her bad mood, Rachel couldn't help feeling a frisson of excitement as she watched Mandy scroll through all the pages of BDSM-related sites.

"Look, here's a site listing the top ten UK BDSM dating sites. Perfect." Mandy clicked the mouse and Rachel leaned over to take a closer look as the homepage popped up in front of them. It looked okay—professional and well researched, and it listed all the pros and cons of the featured sites.

"What about that one?" asked Rachel, pointing to the site

at number three, which was reviewed as being the most user-friendly. Mandy clicked the link to the website and the homepage that flashed up onto the screen looked sexy without being too intimidating. *So far, so good.*

"Okay, you've got to register before you can go any further so think of a username," ordered Mandy, giving Rachel a quick glance. Rachel, who was beginning to feel the warm, fuzzy effects of the wine, grinned and tried to think of something sexy and naughty.

"How about SpankMeNow?" she giggled. "Or FuckThisSub."

"Don't be stupid." Mandy gave her a hard stare and turned back to the computer screen. "This could be the beginning of something special and if you should meet a gorgeous Dom, you don't want him thinking you're some silly little girl who isn't taking this seriously. Now, think again and this time, be sensible."

"Yes, Miss!" Rachel raised her hand in a mock salute and tried to refocus her brain on a slightly more appropriate username. "How about RachelSub? That won't leave any doubt about my name or preference."

"Okay, that'll do." Mandy busied herself creating the account for Rachel and when she finally clicked on the return confirmation email, the account was ready. "Right, all you have to do is post a photo of yourself and write a couple of short sentences about what you're looking for. You can fill in your profile bio another time."

Ten minutes later, Mandy and Rachel sat back and studied the new complete profile. The photo they'd used had been taken about two months earlier at a party. The picture flattered her slim, petite figure, and her long, blonde hair looked sleek and sexy.

"I think that's about it," said Mandy, reaching out to pour herself another glass of wine only to find the bottle empty. "Bloody hell, Rach, you finished the wine. Anyway, let me read your bio out to you and if you want to change anything just stop me. Okay?"

Rachel nodded drunkenly as Mandy started reading, "'I'm a twenty-eight-year-old girl from London who is looking to explore her sexuality with a fun but firm Dom. I'm new to BDSM and hope to meet a sensitive, patient man, in his late twenties or thirties, who will show me the ropes — pun intended'!"

"Are you happy with that?" Mandy raised her eyebrows at Rachel, who was looking worried.

"Shit, Mandy. What if someone actually responds?" whispered Rachel, feeling a twinge of apprehension deep in her stomach.

"Well, that is the general idea." Mandy rolled her eyes and clicked the save button.

Suddenly, the idea that her fantasies may become real seemed terrifying. After all, fantasies were safe and she could control them, but a real life Dom? A shiver ran through her and she reluctantly acknowledged a feeling of delicious anticipation rather than doubt.

"There, it's done. Now we wait and see if anyone sends you a message. Let's see if there's anyone interesting in the recommended search." Mandy winked at Rachel and they both shifted their chairs a little closer to the computer.

They started scrolling down the long list of potential Doms. The first one they looked at sounded like a right wimp —

I'm a 25-year-old straight man. Want to meet a nice girl who will let me tie her up.

His picture didn't exactly do him any favors either, he looked around sixteen and about as dominant as a kitten.

The next one was the complete opposite of the first —

Strict Dom wants compliant sub to train. Must be willing to submit 24/7.

The man in the photo looked like an ax-murderer. Rachel glanced at Mandy, who gave her a nervous smile. This wasn't exactly what she had been expecting.

The next one was even scarier —

I'll tie you up and whip you till you beg me to fuck your tight little arse.

The guy in the photo actually looked fairly normal, which made him seem even more terrifying.

"Bloody hell, Mandy, what have we done? I should never have agreed to this." Rachel felt panic setting in as she imagined being stalked by wicked sadists and big, bad Doms.

"Chill out, Rach. There's no way people will be able to see your contact details. My advice is to sleep on it tonight and tomorrow we'll check if there are any messages in your mailbox. If you don't like the look of any of them just click the decline button and wait until you hear from someone you do like the look of." Rachel fiddled nervously with her hair and watched as Mandy pushed her chair away from the computer and fixed her gaze on her.

"Okay, babe, you're pissed and have to face the boss from hell in the morning so you'd better get something to eat before you go to bed."

"Thanks for reminding me," groaned Rachel, suddenly feeling deflated again. The last thing she wanted was to go to bed where her imagination would undoubtedly run riot. "I've got a much better idea. Let's go to the pub and get pissed out of our heads."

Mandy stood up and stretched. "Tell you what, we'll go to the pub for one quick drink and then stop off at the takeaway on the way back. Come on, slap a bit of lippy on, girl."

"God, you're so domineering," said Rachel with a grin, feeling her spirits begin to lift again. "It's a shame we're not gay, because you'd make a great Domme."

* * * *

27

"Rachel! Come here, please," Adam Stone's voice bellowed as Rachel took her jacket off. She pulled a face and stuck her tongue out at his door. She had hoped he wouldn't be in yet or would have at least given her a few minutes to get settled before he began his attack.

"Yes, Mr Stone," she called back and headed into his office with all the enthusiasm she could muster.

"I'd like a word. Would you bring me a coffee first, though." It wasn't a request, it was an order. "And bring one for yourself."

Oh God, this sounded serious. "Yes, Sir," she answered. She couldn't meet his eyes so she lowered hers and looked at the floor, but not before she noticed a very faint smile on his lips.

Once safely in the privacy of the small kitchen, she buried her head in her hands, wishing she could go home. She'd rather have been anywhere else at that point as, apart from having to face Mr Stone again, she was also nursing a very sore head. The one drink at the pub last night had, of course, turned into several and it had been eleven o'clock before they had finally stumbled out of the pub, bypassing the takeaway and instead stopping off at the late night off-license on their way home.

With a bottle of wine in her bag and all her woes forgotten, Rachel had loudly sung a song by Nine Inch Nails she'd heard a few times — something about meeting your master — and Mandy had had to threaten her with a spanking if she didn't quiet down. This had reduced them both to tears of laughter as they'd crawled up the stairs to the flat on their hands and knees. They'd tried very hard to be quiet as they'd made their way up, but the more they'd tried, the more they'd giggled until they'd both collapsed on the landing, holding their stomachs from laughing so much.

Once safely inside the flat, Rachel had opened the wine, a screw top this time, and poured them a huge glass each while Mandy had logged on to the computer to see if Rachel had any messages on the BDSM site yet.

"Oh my God," Mandy had squealed, "you've got eight messages already. Come and see."

And they had sat up until two o'clock finishing the wine and laughing at the messages, none of which warranted a response. A couple of them sounded okay, but only okay, and the rest were downright scary. One of them was demanding a slave and another wanted a Domme to dominate him, but also wanted a female sub that he in turn could dominate.

"You could do that," Rachel had giggled to Mandy, who had then practically fallen out of her chair, laughing.

"Yeah, so you'd better watch out, sub."

"Seriously, hon," Rachel had said, trying her best not to slur her words too much. "You'd make a great Domme, you're so bossy."

"Thank you very much," Mandy had laughed. "Tell you what, if you don't end up meeting someone, I could always spank you with the hairbrush if it makes you happy."

"Ooh, I nearly forgot to tell you, Mr Stone threatened to spank me today." Rachel had felt a surge of heat shoot through her body at the memory of his words. Just imagining Adam Stone spanking her had been enough to make her horny—until she'd remembered that she hated him.

"You're joking?" Mandy had stared at her friend in shock.

"Nope. He said that in different circumstances he'd put me over his knee." Rachel had then held up her glass and tried to focus her eyes on Mandy, who seemed to have developed a double. "I don't think I was meant to have heard it, but I did."

Their conversation had then descended into complete smut and they had both eventually fallen asleep in each other's arms on the sofa, only waking up when they'd heard Mandy's alarm clock ringing loudly from her bedroom.

Dragging herself out of her drunken sleep, Rachel had been seriously tempted to call in sick. In fact, if she'd been working for Joe she would have, but even through the foggy haze in her head she'd realized that Adam Stone would never let her get away with that. Just the thought of him made her feel sick and it had taken all her strength, along with some painkillers, to make herself presentable enough to meet his standards.

How the hell am I going to get through today? She switched on the coffee machine and tried to ignore the pounding in her head. He'd said he wanted a word. Shit, what did that mean? Was he about to fire her? Maybe that wasn't such a bad thing—at least she would be able to go home and get some sleep, with the huge advantage that she'd never have to see him again.

Five minutes later, she stopped outside his office and took a deep breath to steady herself. She looked down at the two steaming cups of coffee she was holding and willed her hands to stop shaking. She felt like a kitten about to come face to face with an angry Rottweiler, and it was with a heavy heart that she fixed a false smile on her face and prepared to face the wrath of Adam Stone.

Chapter Four

Mr Stone was on the phone when she entered his office and he nodded briefly at the chair opposite his desk, instructing her to sit. She remembered the coasters this time, although she was sorely tempted to put the mugs straight onto the desk just to wind him up. If he was going to fire her anyway, she might as well fight back in some way.

But the tiny dose of defiance didn't last long and she obediently sat down and waited for him to finish his call so he could begin his onslaught. As she waited, eyes downcast, she felt strangely calmed by the sound of his voice – so deep, velvety and sexy. He pronounced his words as if each one had a special meaning, placing nuances and expression in all the right places. In fact, his voice and articulation reminded her a bit of the Shakespearean actor and *Star Trek* captain Patrick Stewart.

She lifted her eyes and stole a quick glance at him while he was facing the window to the side of the desk. What was it about him that turned her into such a quivering wreck? Well, apart from his good looks of course. She studied his perfect face, the slight kink in his nose only adding to the beautiful masculinity of his face. She had come across handsome men before, plenty of them, but none with that extra 'something' that Adam Stone had. What was it? Charm? Yes, definitely, although she had yet to be on the receiving end of it. Nevertheless, he undoubtedly possessed it in abundance. But it was something more than that.

Suddenly, Mr Stone turned back to face her and she quickly diverted her eyes back down to the carpet. Why the hell couldn't she look him in the eye? Yes, she was scared to death of him, but she wasn't normally such a wimp. She'd squared up to much scarier men than him before, her strong will easily winning her arguments, so why did he have this effect on her?

Mr Stone exchanged final pleasantries on the phone before hanging up and returning his attention to her. "Sorry about that."

His smooth voice lured her momentarily into a false sense of security—he certainly didn't sound like he was going to tear strips off her and fire her. "Rachel, look at me," he commanded, as she continued to stare down at the nondescript carpet.

Bastard, she thought, and slowly raised her eyes to meet his. She involuntarily shifted slightly in her chair as his eyes met hers. A stray lock of hair had come loose from the chignon she had struggled with that morning, and she nervously tucked it behind her ear. She took a deep breath and braced herself for the verbal assault.

"I owe you an apology." His voice was calm and smooth with no trace of anger.

What? She was so unprepared for this that she just stared stupidly at him for a moment or two before his words started sinking in. Shit, what should she say? Was he trying to trap her by being nice before he suddenly went in for the kill?

Mr Stone sat back in his chair and smiled, a natural, friendly smile that sent little butterflies fluttering deep down in her stomach. "I was completely out of order yesterday. I'd had a bad start to the day, then I got the call from Lucy and on top of that my ex-wife was giving me grief."

Someone actually dared to give him grief? God, she was brave. Rachel finally smiled back at him, relaxing as she accepted that he wasn't still mad at her. "That's all right," she said, as evenly as she could, considering that her insides felt like they had been put through a spin cycle.

"No, it's not all right. You were helping me out, without notice, and I took my bad mood out on you. That was unfair and unprofessional of me." His eyes, which had seemed so cold and hard yesterday, were warm and sincere. The spin cycle picked up speed.

"You must have been pretty mad when you found out about Lucy," muttered Rachel, trying to find an excuse on his behalf.

Adam Stone frowned. "Is that what you think of me? Christ, I must have been a complete shit yesterday." Shaking his head, he fixed his eyes on her, demanding that she held his gaze. "Of course I wasn't mad, I was worried. Lucy and Pete are very special to me so when I heard that Lucy had pre-eclampsia I was extremely concerned."

"Oh." Rachel looked away, now ashamed for thinking so badly of him.

"That's why I wasn't here when you turned up yesterday," he continued. "I'd popped down to the florists in Covent Garden to order her some flowers—I wanted to choose them myself."

Rachel tried to imagine Adam Stone in a florist shop personally picking flowers to make up a beautiful bouquet. The image couldn't have been further from the one she'd had just five minutes ago. She smiled at him and felt a warm flush run through her body.

"Do you accept my apology?"

"Yes, of course." How could she not accept the apology of a man who personally chose the flowers for his PA's bouquet? She fiddled nervously with her hands in her lap, unsure of what to say or do next.

"Good, thank you." He smiled again, one that easily reached his eyes and made his dimples reappear. "Now, do you have any plans at lunchtime?"

Oh, was he going to make her work through lunch? Her head was still sore and she badly needed some food to help soak up the remainder of last night's alcohol. With an effort not to look too upset, she shook her head. "No, Sir."

"Good. Mirage is already booked so we'll leave just before twelve thirty." Then his tone changed again, returning to the stern and detached voice she was getting used to. "Now, about your shorthand, or, rather, lack of it. Do you audio type?"

Rachel nodded, mutely. Lunch? Had she got that right? Was he taking her to lunch?

"Good, I had rather hoped you could, so I dictated a tape this morning." Without another word he handed her a small tape and inclined his head toward the door, curtly dismissing her.

Back at her desk, Rachel still wasn't sure if she had heard right. Had he just said he was taking her to lunch? Maybe he was just reminding her that he was meeting a client for lunch to make her check the online diary. That would be it—he was probably having a little dig at her because of her fuck-up yesterday.

As she fired up the computer, she glanced quickly at her mobile and saw there was a text waiting for her. It was from Mandy.

Did the bastard fire you? Let me know what happened. M xx

Grinning, Rachel quickly keyed her reply, *No, he apologized! Will talk tonight. R x*

A couple of minutes later, her phone bleeped again.

Sorry, not home tonight. Out with girls from work, will be late. M xx

Oh well never mind, she thought, as she put on the headphones and lost herself in Adam Stone's beautiful voice as she started typing.

The morning passed quickly with no dramas. Adam Stone remained courteous and polite and didn't seem to have any complaints about her work. At twenty-five past twelve, he strode out of his office and nodded at her. "Are you ready?"

Oh God, he really was taking her to lunch! "Er, yes," she

stuttered, and quickly grabbed her bag.

Ten minutes later, they were seated in a busy, modern restaurant frequented mostly by business people.

"Mr Stone, very good to see you." The tall, rather attractive maître d' rushed over to their table and shook Mr Stone's hand like an old friend before turning to Rachel and giving her a warm smile. "Have you replaced the lovely Lucy?" he asked, laughing.

Mr Stone smiled back at him. "Hello, Pierre. This is Rachel. Unfortunately, Lucy has taken ill so Rachel is helping out until the new maternity cover starts."

Pierre's face fell. "I'm very sorry to hear that. Please send her my best wishes."

"Thank you." Mr Stone took the menus Pierre was holding out to him and, without opening them, asked Rachel, "Do you eat fish?"

"Yes, but…"

"Good. Pierre, we'll have two lemon soles with buttered new potatoes and wilted spinach."

Rachel had been about to say that she didn't fancy fish, but it looked like she wasn't going to be given a choice. Oh well, luckily she liked lemon sole. Then, just as she was wondering whether to have a Diet Coke or a lemonade, Mr Stone ordered two glasses of sparkling water for them. *Bloody hell*, she thought crossly, *he could have asked*.

"Is there a problem?" Mr Stone was staring at her and she realized she must have been frowning. She quickly smoothed out her expression and replaced her disgruntled expression with a smile.

"No, of course not."

"Good. I come here every two weeks with Lucy," he said. "It gives us a chance to catch up without interruptions. I like to keep in touch with my employees—it makes for better working relationships."

"I think that's a great idea," said Rachel, thinking briefly that if this was how he encouraged his working relationships, she'd love to see what he was like with his private relationships. *Stop it, Rachel,* she scolded herself and forced her attention back to the man opposite her.

Mr Stone leaned back in his seat and studied Rachel silently before asking, "Do you enjoy working for Joe?"

"Yes, he's a good boss, we work well together." She thanked the waitress as she placed a glass of icy sparkling water in front of her.

"How long have you worked for him?" Mr Stone was looking at her in a way that made her feel incredibly self-conscious. His sharp eyes clearly didn't miss a thing and she wondered if he could read all her expressions and mannerisms. She knew a lot of successful business people studied body language so they could assess people's reactions, and the thought made her uncomfortable. What if he knew that she fancied him like mad at the same time as hating him? Mind you, that probably wasn't an unusual occurrence for him.

She looked up at his face and saw him waiting expectantly for her answer. Shit, she'd gotten distracted—again.

"About six years, I think," she said, before taking a sip of the water, knowing full well that he would already have known the answer.

"There's something I don't understand about you, Rachel," he said, thoughtfully. "You're obviously a very bright woman, your qualifications are excellent and you come across as articulate and personable, if not a little scatty."

Do I?

"And yet," he continued, "you don't seem very ambitious. You've had several opportunities to move on at Stone Media and you're still in the same position you were in six years ago. Why?"

Rachel didn't bother to hide her frown this time. What the hell was wrong with having the same job for six years? It showed dedication and loyalty for God's sake. "Mr Stone," she said, coolly, "how long have you been CEO of Stone Media?"

36

There was mirth in his eyes as he answered, "Eight years."

"And why are you still CEO? Why haven't you sold the company or made yourself Chairman or whatever?" she demanded, angrily.

"I am Chairman."

"Oh. Well, you know what I mean. Just because I'm a lowly secretary doesn't mean that I'm not successful. I choose to stay in my job because I enjoy it, I like Joe and I like the stability. If I wanted to move up the corporate ladder, I would have done so, so please don't write me off as a complete loser."

Ha, that told him. It was true, she was happy with her job — it paid the bills and allowed her the freedom to have fun outside work. Every year, at her appraisal, some jumped-up smart-arse from HR would ask her where she'd like to be in a year's time and her answer was always the same — to still be doing her present job to the best of her ability.

"So it's not because of a lack of confidence?" probed Mr Stone, his gaze never leaving her face.

"Of course not." Rachel looked down at the table to try to hide the surge of heat staining her cheeks because Mr Stone had just seen right through her bravado and had her completely sussed. Yes, it was true that she was happy in her job, but actually she didn't have a lot of confidence and she knew that one of the reasons she never applied for more senior positions was because she was scared she would screw up. The memory of Joe's Genoa trip was testament to that, along with her disastrous day yesterday.

"Rachel" — Mr Stone's voice was gentle — "I wasn't trying to catch you out or to imply there's anything wrong with being a secretary, I'd be lost without one, for God's sake. I like to know who I'm working with, so I wanted to try to get to know what your thoughts and ambitions are, that's all." His lips curled into a mischievous smile as he added, "We'll work on your confidence issues another time."

Rachel was about to insist that she did not have any confidence issues when the waitress brought their food.

Thankfully, that was the end of the subject.

The fish was delicious. Mr Stone had been right in ordering it—she'd never have thought to try it and would have missed out on a fabulous meal. They exchanged small talk as they ate, mostly tidbits about the office, but, even though he was relaxed, Rachel had a feeling that Mr Stone was constantly assessing her, working out what she was thinking before she probably even thought it herself.

When they were finished, he sat back and ran his eyes lazily over her body. She felt herself turn a deep puce and moved uncomfortably in her chair.

"Dessert?" he asked.

"Oh, no thanks." She smiled, and took another sip of water.

"Can we see the dessert menu?" he asked the waitress, as she cleared their table.

"Yes, of course." She smiled, and fluttered her eyelashes at him.

Rachel stifled a giggle. The girl was actually flirting with her boss. Then she blushed when she remembered all the times she must have fluttered her eyelashes at him herself. Shit, she hadn't realized it was so obvious.

The young girl came back with a menu and handed it to Mr Stone. He glanced at it briefly and returned his gaze to Rachel, eyebrows slightly furrowed, as if he were contemplating something.

"Do you prefer vanilla," he murmured, "or are you more adventurous?"

"Sorry?" Rachel felt her cheeks burn as she tried to appear innocently oblivious to the inferred nature of his question.

"Ice cream. Do you prefer plain, predictable vanilla or would you like to try something a bit more exotic and interesting like passion fruit sorbet?" Mr Stone's face remained completely straight and Rachel suddenly realized he must have been talking about ice cream all along. Oh God, she'd thought he was asking about her sexual preferences. What was wrong with her?

"I'm fine, thank you," she managed to reply. "I really don't need a dessert."

"She'll try the sorbet," said Mr Stone, and handed the waitress the menu. "I'll just have a coffee."

"Mr Stone, I really don't..." Rachel's voice trailed off when she caught his icy eyes glaring at her. She was clearly going to have the sorbet whether she liked it or not. "Are you always so bossy?" she grumbled under her breath.

"Yes, Rachel," he replied, his voice soft, but with a dark undertone. "One day you'll learn that I will always know what you want, even before you do, and when that time comes you'll obey me without question. Do you understand?"

"Yes, Sir," she whispered. Wow—did he know about her BDSM fantasies, and if so was he making a pass at her or was he just talking about her choices of food? His words could be taken in either context and she sighed in relief as the waitress brought her dessert so she could concentrate on tucking into it rather than thinking about the hot, throbbing sensation growing between her legs.

Chapter Five

At six o'clock, with all her work up to date and the phone finally quiet, Rachel logged off her computer and cleared the last couple of things from her desk. She glanced at Mr Stone's closed door and felt a nervous twitch settle into a hard lump in her stomach.

Did she dare knock on the door and risk disturbing him? Should she ask if she could leave or should she just slip out without bothering him? Yesterday, he'd told her she could go, but his door had been open so he obviously hadn't been too busy. Did the fact that his door was closed now mean 'Do Not Disturb'?

The trouble was, she needed to talk to him and even though it would probably really annoy him to be disturbed for something so trivial, it was important to her and she needed an answer.

So, with a shaking hand, she knocked gently on his door and waited.

"Yes?" He sounded annoyed.

She peeped nervously around the door and gave him a shaky smile, which was futile as he didn't even look up from his laptop. "Er, Mr Stone? I was wondering if I could have a word, please?"

He finally looked up and actually smiled at her. "What can I do for you, Rachel?" He didn't sound annoyed at all, she realized with relief. The thought made her feel a bit braver as she made her way over to his desk and waited to be invited to sit.

When he didn't say anything, she remained standing and cleared her throat. "I was just wondering if…if you have any idea how long I'll be working for you. Not that I mind," she said, hastily. "It would just be helpful to know."

Mr Stone's eyes darkened and a look of anger crossed his face as he glared at her in disbelief. Oh shit, she wished she hadn't said anything now.

"Didn't HR fill you in?" he asked, with an edge to his voice that made her want to run out of his office and hide.

"No, Sir. I'm sorry, you're right, I should have spoken to them first."

"No, Rachel. That's not good enough, you shouldn't have to chase them. I asked them yesterday to let you know the terms of this arrangement." He picked up his phone and punched a key. "Jason?" he said, after a couple of seconds. "Who's in charge of organizing Lucy's replacement?" He waited in silence as Jason checked his files. "Thanks," he growled. "Send him up to my office, *now*."

He slammed the phone down and ran a hand roughly through his hair. "Rachel, I'm very sorry that no one has spoken to you about this. I've had a temporary contract drawn up with details of your new pro rata salary and working hours. I don't know the exact date Lucy's maternity cover was due to start, but I know she was roughly three months away from going on leave."

"Thank you, Sir." She started to turn so she could retreat back to the safety of her own office, but Mr Stone called her back.

"Sit down!" His voice had the same angry tone as yesterday, but she felt comforted by the knowledge that it wasn't her he was pissed off with. Still, she didn't particularly want to witness some poor sod getting hauled over the coals because of her. She sat down as instructed, automatically casting her eyes downwards, and waited in an uncomfortable silence for the HR guy to arrive. She glanced up at Mr Stone briefly, but wished she hadn't when she saw his tightly clenched jaw and furrowed brow.

She heard the lift ping in the hall and a few seconds later, someone knocked softly on the door. "Mr Stone?"

"Michael!" Mr Stone gestured for the young man to approach. Rachel, feeling really sorry for the poor guy, looked back down at the floor and wished she was somewhere else. Michael looked ashen, she could see his hands trembling slightly as he stood before the large desk. He knew he was in trouble.

"Were you given the job of organizing Lucy's replacement when she was taken ill yesterday?" Mr Stone's voice sounded steady, but deadly, and Rachel felt Michael's fear.

"Yes, Mr Stone," whispered Michael, wiping his hands on the back of his trousers.

"Did Jason ask you to make sure Miss Porter was given a copy of the temporary contract?"

"Well, the thing is Mr…" Michael's voice faltered.

"Yes or no?" snapped Mr Stone.

Michael's face was now flushed a deep red. "Yes. I'm sorry, I needed to check some dates and by the time it was ready last night, Miss Porter had left. I was going to send it up first thing this morning but…"

Mr Stone's voice was very quiet when he cut Michael off, but it was way more intimidating than it would have been if he'd shouted. "I don't know what the hell you guys down there do all day, but I will *not* tolerate such incompetence. Get me that contract *now* and the next time I come across your name it had better not have anything to do with negligence. Now get out!"

As Rachel watched Michael scurry out of the office, she felt awful. This was all her fault. If only she hadn't said anything, Michael would probably have left the contract on her desk in the morning and Adam Stone would have been none the wiser. She was also painfully aware that it was very likely she would also be on the receiving end of his rage at some point as she was bound to screw up at least once in the next three months. Yesterday had proved that.

"Please don't be too hard on him, Mr Stone," she pleaded. "I'm sure it was only an oversight."

Mr Stone shot her an angry look. "There's no excuse for

incompetence, Rachel. If someone's not capable of such a simple task without screwing it up, they don't belong at Stone Media."

Oh great, that's me gone then. She fiddled nervously with her bracelet and tried to look unconcerned.

As if reading her mind, he gave her an intense stare and added softly, "Don't look so worried. I think you'll find that I discipline my staff fairly, unless of course..." He raised an eyebrow leaving the unfinished sentence to speak for itself. She had a quick flashback to his words yesterday, something about putting her over his knee.

Oh. My. God. Burning heat rushed to her cheeks as she digested his words. He gave her a subtle smile when he saw her flush and she knew she had just given the game away by reacting the way she had. His dark eyes continued scrutinizing her and she quickly averted her own eyes to the window behind him. He didn't say anything else, clearly not bothered by the uncomfortable silence, but for her it was unbearable. Every second that passed felt more difficult as it became harder not to return her gaze to him. She coughed softly and focused her attention on a smudge on the window as minutes ticked endlessly by.

Thankfully, Michael returned, apologizing profusely as he handed the contract over to Mr Stone, who then had the grace to thank Michael for bringing it up. Michael, still flushed, made his exit as quickly as he could and Rachel made a mental note to pop down to HR tomorrow to personally say how sorry she was about the whole stupid incident.

She read the contract through, signed it and thanked Mr Stone before saying goodnight and making her own hasty exit. She needed to get out of the office, away from Adam Stone as quickly as possible. The man terrified her, and yet she was so damned attracted to him.

* * * *

Back home, Rachel made herself a bowl of cheese and tomato pasta and settled onto the sofa to watch *EastEnders*. It was quite nice having the flat to herself for once – it gave her time to think. Think about Adam Stone. How did he seem to know her so well? He'd been dead right when he'd picked up on her lack of confidence earlier, which had surprised her because she'd thought she hid it pretty well. Her lips hardened into a thin line, but she quickly swallowed any thoughts of bitterness and resolved not to discuss her past with him if she could get away with it.

Her mind drifted back to their lunch and the way he had asked about her preferences for ice cream and had firmly told her that, in time, she would obey him without question. Wow, that was the sort of thing a Dom would say, wasn't it? She smiled as she imagined him standing over her, flogger in hand, demanding she do all sorts of delicious things to his body, and was immediately rewarded with a rush of dampness between her legs. Hmm, Adam Stone would make a shit-hot Dom. Scary, but very sexy.

Thinking of scary Doms reminded her of the website she'd joined yesterday. She hadn't yet checked to see if there were any new messages and the thought that someone might have liked her profile enough to want to contact her sent a bolt of excitement through her. She jumped up from the sofa and quickly made her way over to the bright pink computer desk.

The computer seemed to take forever to fire up, but finally she was on the page Mandy had bookmarked for her the day before. She typed in her password and held her breath as she waited for her profile page to show up and when it did, she gasped in delight as she saw there were sixteen new messages for her.

She quickly scrolled through the list and was immediately able to disregard about half of them. Like last night, a lot of them were either too scary or just plain weird.

The first of the remaining messages she clicked on was from someone called JSP0171.

Hi, Rachel, you sound delectable. Please send me some pics of yourself without your clothes on.

Yeah, right, you perv, she thought, and deleted it without reading any further. The next one was from HotTash.

Hello. I know you said you wanted a man but if you fancy a hot, sexy Domme then let me know.

"No, when I said I wanted a man, I meant I wanted a man, you silly cow," she grumbled, and deleted that one as well. Oh, dear, this wasn't going to be as easy as she had first thought.

The next one sounded a bit more promising.

Hi there, my name's Ted. I'm 34 and a teacher from Croydon. Would love to show u the scene so if u r interested pls get in touch. The next local Munch is next week so if you'd like to come along and meet some of our crowd, I'd love to bring u as my guest.

Rachel smiled as she looked at his picture. He didn't look particularly scary or weird so she put him into her favorites and decided he might be worth a reply.

The next three weren't that interesting so she deleted them straight away, which only left two more. She clicked on the first of the two.

Hi Rachel, I've just seen your profile and picture and I must say, you look gorgeous, I love blondes! I've always been a Dom, but my last girlfriend of two years was definitely vanilla, so, now that I'm a free agent again, I'm looking to rediscover my Dominant side. I would love to meet someone like yourself, who is new to the scene so we can learn and grow together, so if you think you might be interested in chatting, I'd be delighted to hear from you. All the best, Luke, Notting Hill.

The picture in the profile was of a good-looking, dark-skinned man in his thirties. This was more like it. Rachel grinned and marked him as a favorite – she would definitely reply to him.

The last one was a young boy of nineteen who was looking for a female sub to train him up as a Dom. She quickly declined that one. That left the two in her favorites, Ted and Luke. They both sounded nice so she decided to reply to both of them and see if they came back to her. She giggled at the thought that she might actually get to meet a real Dom who could finally make her fantasies come true.

She quickly started typing a reply to Ted in Croydon.

Hi Ted, Thanks for your reply and for your invitation to your local Munch – sorry, but what's a Munch?

She wrote a bit about herself and ended the message by saying she hoped to hear back from him soon.

Next was Luke. She really liked the sound of him and he was cute too.

Hi Luke, she wrote, *Thank you for your message. It was a pleasant change to receive a message from someone who sounds normal and sane. I must admit I've had some pretty strange responses!*

She decided to be completely straight with this guy – she had a feeling he would appreciate it and if he didn't, then she didn't have anything to lose.

I live in North London with my flatmate – it's thanks to her that I've finally had the courage to join this site. I've had fantasies about finding a Dom for a while now, but this is the first time I've acted on it and I must admit, it's a bit scary. My only experience of BDSM is from the Internet so I'm afraid I'm a complete novice. I'd love to hear more about you so if I haven't just scared you off then I'll look forward to hearing back from you. Rachel. X

She had no idea if that was the sort of thing you were supposed to write in response to these posts, but it would have to do and if he didn't like her, then tough. She clicked send.

With the dating site done, she decided to do a bit more reading up on BDSM and found a great site titled, 'What Makes A Good Sub?' She found herself becoming more and more turned on as she read the article and could completely identify with the author. It certainly left her more certain than ever that she really was a submissive and all this wasn't just some passing phase.

Finally, she stood up, stretched and checked the time. Shit, it was nearly midnight. She'd been on the computer for over three hours. With a yawn, she logged off and made her way to the bathroom, wondering idly what time Mandy would be back. Not that she was that bothered, as long as Mandy was quiet when she came back so she wouldn't wake her. She needed all the beauty sleep she could get so she wouldn't have to face Adam Stone tomorrow with bags under her eyes. Thinking about him made her smile and it was with sexy thoughts of him that she drifted off to sleep within five minutes of crawling under her duvet.

"Pull your knickers down." The order was clear and Rachel felt a thrill shoot through her as she slowly lowered her knickers to her ankles.

"Good girl, now get across my knee. Now!" The voice was deep and commanding.

"Yes, Sir," she said, and quickly laid herself over his knees. She felt his hand, so strong and large, caressing her bare cheeks. "Hmm, that feels sooo good, Sir."

"Are you sorry you disobeyed me?"

"Yes, Sir." His hand landed on her right arse cheek with a loud, stinging blow.

Ouch!

"How sorry?"

"Very sorry, Sir." Slap – another blow, this time harder than the first. Her clit was throbbing hard now and she tried to shift herself on his knee to see if the friction might rub against it.

"Did I say you could move?"

"No, I'm sorry, Sir." Another slap, even harder. Her arse was

47

beginning to burn and it felt so deliciously sexy that she nearly came.

"Don't you dare come until I say you can," the man growled.

"Please, Sir, can I come now?" The throbbing was becoming unbearable and as his hand came down again in a loud, heavy slap, her body surrendered and she knew she wouldn't be able to stop herself from coming.

"Oh, shit," she groaned, as she slowly woke and acknowledged that, once again, it had all been a dream. Only this time it was different, she realized, as a smile spread across her face. This time her fantasy lover had had a face. She closed her eyes again and recalled the image of the man who had so mercilessly spanked her in her dream. The face of Adam Stone.

Chapter Six

It was gone two o'clock in the morning and Rachel was alone and very aroused—again! Normally she'd reach for the Rabbit but, for once, she didn't think it would be enough. Besides, she still hadn't gotten round to replacing the batteries. No, what she needed was a real man, Adam Stone ideally, but seeing as that wasn't possible, the next best thing would be to see if either Ted or Luke had responded to her messages.

She tiptoed through the flat, carefully stepping over Mandy's coat and shoes, which had been carelessly strewn across the hallway floor, and made her way to the computer. She was wide awake now and knew she wouldn't be able to sleep for a least another couple of hours. She might as well use the time to search for more information on BDSM while she had a bit of privacy. Maybe she could find some erotic BDSM novels to download onto her e-reader—she would be able to read them anywhere and no one would know what she was doing. She grinned as she imagined reading about raunchy Doms in their dungeons while on the Tube going to work. There were advantages to owning an e-reader.

She logged on to the dating site and saw there were three new messages. Two of them were from people she didn't know—she'd get to them later—and the third was from Luke, the cute one. With an excited grin spreading over her face, she clicked on his message and read—

Hi, Rachel, Thanks for your reply and no, you haven't scared me off. In fact, I like your directness, that's very refreshing. You're right about some of the people on here — sometimes I wonder if they're really real or just kids having a laugh. You mention you haven't yet had any experience with BDSM, do you mind if I ask what made you think it was something you might want to explore? Hope to hear from you again. Luke x

Rachel couldn't stop smiling as she re-read the message. Luke sounded really nice and she couldn't wait to hear more from this potential Dom. She quickly typed a reply.

Hi, Luke. Thanks for your message. I don't mind you asking at all and I'm very happy to tell you more about myself. I've been single for just over a year — please don't ask about that — and have recently been having some very vivid dreams where I've been tied up and spanked by a gorgeous man. I've been doing a bit of research on BDSM and feel that I've finally found something that has been missing from my life — does that sound corny? Rachel X

Once she'd pressed send, she decided to make herself a mug of tea before looking on Amazon to check out some saucy novels. She wondered what Luke was doing now — probably asleep as it was nearly half past two in the morning. Would he check his inbox when he woke up in the morning or would he wait and reply when he got back from work? If he replied at all, of course. With her tea made, she sat back down in front of the computer and was about to leave the site when she noticed a new message.

It was a reply from Luke.

Hi Gorgeous, What are you doing up at this time of night? Don't you sleep?

Grinning, she quickly typed, *Hi, I could say the same about you! I couldn't sleep! Rx*

Why, did you have another dream?

Lol, how did you guess?

Wish I could help you with that!

Ooh, this is so bloody sexy, she thought in delight. She decided to throw caution to the wind and replied, *So do I!!*

A few seconds later and a reply came back, *It sounds like you could do with some practical research ;-) If you're free tomorrow night I'd be happy to take you to a BDSM club I know. Nothing heavy, just drinks and a chat and if you're not up for anything else, that's fine. Are you interested?*

Was she interested? Too bloody right she was. Her normally sensible and cautious side had been well and truly buried and her hands were shaking as she typed her reply, *I might be. Where were you thinking of? BTW, I don't normally arrange to meet strange men in kinky nightclubs – just so you know.*

I'm a member of Boundaries, a private BDSM club in South London. I could meet you in Central London at, say 9pm and we could get a cab there together. Oh, and just for the record, I don't normally take strange girls to kinky nightclubs either.

She really liked the sound of this guy, but she knew she was being irresponsible for arranging to meet him without knowing anything about him. He did sound genuine, though, and she had a gut feeling that he was all right.

Lol. Where were you thinking of meeting?

How about by Bond Street Tube Station, I'll recognize you from your photo. Oh, and wear something sexy or they won't let you in.

Sexy? Did she have anything sexy that would get her into a BDSM club? No, but there were advantages to working in Central London – she could nip out at lunchtime.

OK, I'll see you then.

Great. Now, get to bed!

Ooh, how sexy, she thought. Giggling, she replied, *Yes, Sir!! Night night. X.*

Night night x

Logging off the site, it was all Rachel could do not to jump up and down like an excited child at a birthday party. She couldn't believe she had just arranged to meet a complete stranger and let him take her to a nightclub, a BDSM one at that. She needed to talk to someone badly and Mandy was home now, although it was nearly quarter to three in the morning. Taking her life in her hands, she tiptoed into Mandy's room and shook her awake.

"You've done what?" screamed Mandy, a minute later, groggy with sleep and alcohol.

"I'm meeting this guy I met on the site—he's taking me to a BDSM club tomorrow night, isn't that great?" Rachel giggled, and waited for Mandy to share her excitement.

"No, it fucking isn't. You can't just go off meeting complete strangers at dodgy nightclubs. For fuck's sake, Rach, he could be a complete nutter!" Mandy was furious and Rachel could only gape at her in surprise.

"But, Mandy, you were the one who told me to join the site and meet someone," she said, frowning. She felt hurt and a bit bewildered at Mandy's reaction.

"Yes, but not someone you've only been in contact with for five bloody minutes. You don't know anything about him." Mandy dragged herself out of bed and reached for her dressing gown.

"I know enough," said Rachel peevishly, and followed Mandy as she made her way into the kitchen.

"Really? Okay, what does he do for a living?"

Rachel hesitated. "Well, he… All right, I don't know, but that isn't important. I really like him, Mandy."

"You don't bloody know him, Rach. You can't just go off with the first man who offers to give you a spanking."

Rachel sighed in mock defeat. "Yeah, I know. I guess I got caught up in the moment."

Mandy's face softened when she saw the expression on her friend's face. "Look, sweetie, I'm sorry for being so harsh about it, but I care about you. I don't want anything bad to happen to you."

Rachel smiled back and gave Mandy a hug. "I know, thanks. I'll contact him in the morning and tell him I might have been a bit hasty." Rachel turned her back on Mandy then uncrossed her fingers. She hadn't actually said she'd cancel, and anyway, she didn't need Mandy's permission to go. It was flattering that Mandy cared, but sometimes she was so damned bossy that it was better to let her think she'd won the argument. She really did like Luke and had no intention of canceling her date tomorrow evening, no matter what Mandy said.

Mandy seemed happy that she had persuaded Rachel to rethink and passed her a mug of hot chocolate. "Good. Okay, now that you've woken me up in the middle of the bloody night, you can fill me in on all the other messages you've had on the site."

* * * *

Rachel sank into the warm, silky bath water and felt her muscles begin to relax. It was Friday night and she was going to Boundaries with Luke. She couldn't wait. Luckily, Mandy was out so she wouldn't be quizzed about where she was going, although it would be pretty obvious once she was dressed. Mandy was a nurse at a London hospital and worked different shifts, so she rarely knew when she was going to be around or not.

She thought back to earlier that afternoon and cringed as she recalled Mr Stone's words just before she'd left the office. The day had started out all right, it had been relatively quiet as Mr Stone had been out at meetings for most of the day and she'd even been able to nip out to do a bit of shopping at lunchtime. She had found a couple of small alternative boutiques at the back of Neale Street in Covent Garden, and had found everything she needed for her sexy outfit.

When she'd arrived back at the office, Mr Stone still hadn't been back so she'd kept her head down and cleared her workload. But then, just as she had been contemplating sneaking off half an hour early, Mr Stone had returned and asked her to pop into his office. He'd gone over some details for a meeting he wanted her to arrange and had handed her a fresh audio tape, which he'd said she could leave until Monday.

Finally, he'd sat back in his seat and had given her one of those looks that instantly sent blood rushing through her veins. His eyes had then roamed idly over her upper body, stopping at her breasts, before raising them to meet her gaze again. Her nipples had hardened—traitors.

"So, Rachel, are you doing anything nice at the weekend?" His deep, soft voice had teased her ears and Rachel had almost been tempted to tell him where she was going later that night. But, luckily, common sense had kicked in and she'd just smiled and said she had a date, but otherwise was going to enjoy a quiet weekend.

"That's good. Well, have a nice time," he'd said, smiling.

"Thank you." Rachel had then stood up and turned to leave his office when he'd suddenly called her back.

"Oh, by the way..." There'd been a slight edge to his voice that had made her quickly swing back around to face him again.

"Yes, Mr Stone?"

"Just a word of advice. I'm sure you're aware of the rules regarding the use of the company Internet for personal reasons?" He'd been watching her closely and would undoubtedly have seen the red flush that crept slowly up from her neck to the top of her head. "If you absolutely must search for non-work-related material at work, especially if it's of a sexual nature, may I suggest you don't bookmark the page?"

Fuck! Rachel had felt as if the floor had disappeared from under her feet. The flush that had tinted her cheeks a minute earlier had then burned deeply and she'd stood, rooted to the spot as she'd tried to think of something to say. But how could she explain a bookmarked page titled 'BDSM – Discover Your Kinky Side?'

Mr Stone, who had obviously been enjoying her reaction, had then smiled knowingly and said, "Goodnight, Rachel."

"Er... Goodnight, Sir," she'd muttered, and had scurried out of the door as quickly as she could.

Just thinking about it made her toes curl in embarrassment so, lathering her body with vanilla scented soap, she resolved not to think any more about Adam Stone. The fact that he knew about her interest in BDSM mortified her, but she didn't want to spoil tonight by worrying about what he might think of her. She would try to put him out of her mind as best she could and concentrate on her date with Luke.

Little butterflies were fluttering through her stomach every time she thought about what might happen later with Luke. Any doubts she might have had as a result of Mandy's warnings had been quickly dashed that morning when she'd logged on and seen a new message from him.

Hi Gorgeous, I'm pretty sure that you've just logged on to tell me you've changed your mind about tonight because you don't know anything about me. As I would hate for you to have to miss out on a night of kinky fun, I thought I'd provide you with a short bio about myself, as well as my address and contact details. You should pass this information on to your flatmate and, if you haven't already done so, arrange for her to call you at a pre-arranged time tonight so she can check you're okay. If you need to verify any of the details I'm about to give you, I'm sure you'll find plenty of information if you Google my law firm.

He then left information about his background, address, date of birth and occupation before saying that he was looking forward to seeing her later.

Rachel had of course Googled him straight away and had found plenty of information about him on his company's website. He was thirty-two years old and a lawyer, originally from New York, now living in Notting Hill. He was divorced with two teenage children and had graduated from Oxford University with a first class honors degree.

And now, in a couple of hours, she'd be meeting him in person. She slid farther into the warm water, letting it gently massage her breasts, and closed her eyes. What would he be like? Strong, powerful and commanding, like Adam Stone? Her eyes shot open. She didn't want to think about Adam Stone tonight. This was nothing to do with him so trying to compare Luke with him was crazy. No one could live up to Adam Stone so it would be unfair of her to set such high expectations. Even if Luke was half as sexy and dominating as him, she'd be happy.

When the bathwater had cooled, she climbed out of the bath and inspected her newly shaven legs and armpits. Then, when she was dry, she smoothed a sensuous body lotion all over her skin leaving it silky soft and smelling gorgeous. She applied her makeup slowly, taking time to make sure it was perfect. She'd even bought a new lipstick today, a bright 'fuck me now' red that she carefully applied to her lips.

An hour later, she stood in front of the mirror and hardly recognized herself. The short black leather miniskirt she'd bought hugged her bottom, and the matching black corset was laced up tightly, cinching her waist and pushing up her generous breasts. She slipped on a pair of black, very high-heeled patent shoes that made her look much taller than her five foot four and checked that her stockings were straight. Hmm, she didn't look too bad, all things considered. She hoped Luke would agree. She'd backcombed her long blonde hair slightly, giving her an eighties rock chick look, and the image staring back at her in the mirror was definitely befitting of an attractive girl about to make her debut in a BDSM club.

Just then she heard the front door close. Damn, Mandy was back and she'd have to be pretty stupid not to work out where she was going. She stood still listening, and sure enough, almost immediately there was a gentle knock on her bedroom door and Mandy's head peeped round.

"Wow!" she gasped, her eyes looking like they were about to pop out of her head when she saw Rachel. "You look amazing."

"It's not too much, is it?" Rachel turned back to the mirror, worried that she might look too tarty.

"No, you look really hot," laughed Mandy. "So, you're meeting Luke then?"

Rachel nodded. "Look, Mandy, I know you're only looking out for me, but I've made up my mind and I'm going tonight, whether you like it or not."

Mandy walked over to her and put her arms around her. "I know, Rach. I'm sorry for being such a bitch last night. I had no right telling you what to do."

Rachel nodded her acceptance to Mandy's apology. "You were only looking out for me and I appreciate that. I've left a printout of Luke's details on the table to shut you up."

"Okay. Can I call you later to check if you're all right?"

Rachel grinned. "Luke actually suggested you do just that. I'm meeting him at nine o'clock so how about you call at about nine fifteen? We should be in a cab by then."

Mandy nodded and gave Rachel another hug before leaving her to finish getting ready.

Twenty minutes later, Rachel was sitting nervously on the Tube, staring at her reflection in the window opposite. In about fifteen minutes she'd be coming face to face with Luke, and suddenly she wished she was at home in the safety of her flat, sharing a bottle of wine with Mandy and looking at BDSM websites. She closed her eyes and shook her head. What had she been thinking?

Five minutes later, the train pulled into Bond Street Station. She rose slowly from her seat and made her way to the doors. As she stepped onto the platform, a train going in the opposite direction stopped and she was very tempted to run across, jump on it and go back home. She stood on the platform, watching both the trains pulling out before turning toward the escalators.

Would he already be there waiting for her? Would he recognize her? Oh God, why the hell hadn't she listened to Mandy?

When she got to the top, she stepped off the escalator, walked slowly through the ticket barrier then looked tentatively around for Luke. Apart from a couple of teenagers waiting for their friends, there was no one else around. She stood awkwardly by the entrance, trying not to look too conspicuous, which was very difficult seeing that she was wearing heels so high that she could barely keep her balance. Thankful she'd worn a coat over her skimpy outfit. She lifted her arm to check the time on her watch and when she looked up again she found herself face to face with her real-life Dom.

Chapter Seven

Luke was tall, muscular and even better looking than his photo, although still not a patch on Adam Stone. His dark hair was short and his eyes were a deep brown — *I could lose myself in eyes like that,* she thought as she smiled up at him. He took her hand, raised it to his lips and kissed it softly. "You're even more beautiful in real life," he said, his words accentuated with a sexy American accent.

"Thank you." Rachel shifted from one foot to the other and tried to look more confident than she felt. "It's nice to meet you."

He took her hand and led her across the pavement, where a minicab was waiting. "After you," he said, holding the door open for her. As the cab pulled away, she sat back in her seat and looked out of the window, trying to fight her feelings of apprehension. Luke was gorgeous and charming but, even so, she was suddenly having doubts — big ones.

"Are you regretting coming?" he asked softly as if reading her thoughts.

"No, of course not," she lied. "I'm just a bit nervous, that's all."

"That's understandable. If you're uncomfortable at any time just let me know. We'll talk about safe words and rules later, but I want you to know that you're not my prisoner, you can leave any time you like."

"Thank you," she said quietly, looking straight ahead to avoid meeting his gaze.

"Look at me, Rachel," he demanded in a voice that screamed 'Dom'. She melted a little and turned to look at him.

"Good girl. Now, open your coat and let me see what you're wearing."

"Erm, okay." She was feeling self-conscious now and looked up at the glass screen separating the driver from his passengers. His eyes were on the road, but it wouldn't take much for him to glance in his mirror and see what they were doing.

Luke's firm voice cut through her reservations. "Two things, Rachel. First, ignore the driver. Secondly, kindly address me as Sir."

"Yes, Sir," she whispered, and slowly started to unbutton her coat.

When she'd finished fiddling with the last of the buttons, Luke leaned over and pulled the coat open, exposing her leather outfit and the bare, pale flesh of her chest and breasts, pushed up by the corset.

"Very nice," he said, and gently kissed the exposed flesh. "Did you obey me last night?"

"Last night?" Rachel frowned. What the hell was he talking about?

"After we'd arranged to meet, I told you to get to bed." He ran his finger lightly over her corset, sending little shivers of pleasure through her.

She giggled. "That was very sexy, but no, I'm afraid not. Mandy, she's my flatmate, woke up and ended up cross-examining me about you."

"Hmm," he said, playfully, "already disobeying me, huh? I think you might have earned yourself a little punishment later. Have you ever been spanked?"

A shot of electricity ran through Rachel's body and her breathing quickened. "No, Sir," she managed to reply.

"Well, we'll have to see if we can remedy that. So, what did Mandy have to say when you told her you were meeting me tonight?"

"She was really cross with me," said Rachel, smiling. "She told me I shouldn't go off with the first man who offered to give me a spanking."

"She's quite right, of course, but I'm glad she didn't talk you out of it."

"Your email this morning helped."

"I thought it might."

Just then her phone started ringing. *Mandy! It must be nine fifteen.* "Sorry," she said to Luke and pressed answer. "Hi"

"Are you all right?" asked Mandy, her voice anxious.

"Yes, thanks," replied Rachel, quietly. "All's well."

"You sure, hon?"

"Absolutely."

"What's he like?"

Rachel rolled her eyes. "I'll talk to you later."

"Oh yeah, sorry, you can't really talk right now, can you? Okay, sweetie, have fun and be good!"

Smiling, Rachel ended the call and switched her phone to silent. When she'd put it away she turned back to Luke. "Sorry about that."

"Mandy?" he asked, with a grin.

"Yes, we agreed she'd call at nine fifteen."

Luke nodded. "Good. Now, let's go over a few things before we arrive at Boundaries." He leaned down and rummaged in a large bag, retrieving something with shiny buckles on. "Give me your wrists," he ordered.

What? Rachel shrank into her seat. She glanced up at the driver again who quickly diverted his eyes from the mirror back to the road. *Oh, my God, he's watching.* Or maybe he was just checking his rear mirror as any good driver should? She stared pleadingly at Luke's face illuminated by the passing street lights.

"Rachel, I won't say it again, give me your wrists. It's the club's rules that all subs wear cuffs."

Oh. A quick glance told her the driver was still watching the road, so she slowly held up her arms and allowed Luke to buckle soft leather cuffs to her wrists. He checked they weren't too tight and released her hands.

"Good. Now, turn toward me and lift your left leg up to one side of me on the seat and your right leg to the other side."

Rachel stared at Luke in shock. "Why?" she gasped, realizing that would mean her legs would be spread open before him. And what about the driver? It would be blatantly obvious what she was doing and, God forbid, she didn't want to give him a cheap thrill, he might just crash the bloody cab.

"Rachel, just do it." Luke's voice was losing some of its patience now.

Slowly, she turned in her seat and raised her left leg, placing it between the side of his body and the backrest. Then, closing her eyes in dread, she raised her other leg and placed it against the other side of Luke's body. She could feel cool air brushing against the thin, lacy material of her knickers and thought she would probably die of embarrassment right then.

Luke grinned and pulled more cuffs out of his bag, placing one of them around her right ankle and buckling it the way he had with her wrists. He then deftly attached the second cuff to her left ankle, but, thankfully, didn't attach the two together. She glanced nervously up at the driver but he didn't seem to take any notice. But what if he'd looked away just before she'd checked? He'd have seen Luke strapping the cuffs on her ankles with her legs splayed. *Oh, the shame.* She bit back burning tears of humiliation and tried to reassure herself that he was just a random driver whom she'd never see again.

"Stay where you are," Luke ordered, when Rachel started to move her legs back down, desperate to resume a normal sitting position. She bit back an angry retort and forced herself to remain where she was, not daring to look up at the driver.

Luke slowly ran a finger up her leg, over her knee and up the inside of her thigh. Rachel held her breath as arousal soared through her body. She hoped he wouldn't notice how turned on she had suddenly become. But then his finger moved ever so slowly a little farther up and very gently brushed against the material covering her pussy. She let out a small involuntary moan. He could probably feel her dampness through her skimpy knickers and she thanked God the orange colored street lights meant he couldn't see her burning face.

"Very nice." He smiled, removing his hand, leaving her wanting more, but thankful that her embarrassment would finally come to an end. But just as she hoped he would let her put her legs back down, he flashed her a wicked grin, his teeth glowing in the orange shadows, and said, "I want you to touch yourself."

"What?" she cried in disbelief. "No."

Luke leaned closer toward her so their noses were nearly touching and growled, "Rachel, you will do as I say or I'll make you walk into the club naked." He sat back, crossed his arms and said calmly, "Your choice."

Rachel's face was now so hot that her eyes watered from the heat. She knew Luke was probably testing her, but could she really touch herself down there in front of him, and the bloody driver, who would undoubtedly have a good look. She also knew that Luke was serious and if she was going to have to humiliate herself, she'd rather do it in a relatively dark cab with an audience of just two than being made to walk into a busy, well-lit club, stark naked.

So, slowly, she lowered her hands and reached down to touch her damp knickers, still exposed to Luke. She started to rub gently, hoping that would be enough to keep him happy, but he didn't miss anything and said, "Fingers inside, Rachel."

Oh crap. She slid her fingers inside her knickers. She was soaked. She was shocked at how much more aroused she became as she started to rub her throbbing clit, knowing she was being watched by Luke and, possibly, the driver.

Finally, after what seemed like forever, Luke spoke again. "You may stop and put your legs back down now."

"Thank you, Sir," she whispered. She quickly lowered her legs before he changed his mind, all the time looking at the floor — she just couldn't bring herself to look at him.

"Remain facing me." Luke reached back down to his bag and pulled something else out. It was difficult to tell what it was in the dark, but it looked like something that matched the cuffs she was now wearing on her wrists and ankles. He reached out and gently ran his finger across her cheek before running it through her hair.

"Lift your hair for me," he ordered, and she did as she'd been told. "The subject of collars is a difficult one," he said, as he fastened the soft leather around her neck. "A Master doesn't normally collar a sub so early on in their relationship, it's normally a very special and intimate occasion, but I think it would be a good idea for you to wear one tonight." He checked it wasn't too tight and continued, "You're a very beautiful woman, Rachel, and there will be a lot of Doms wanting to play with you tonight, but I don't think you're ready for that just yet. This collar will tell them you're spoken for and will insure you don't get any unwanted attention."

"Thank you, Sir." She lifted her hand and ran her fingers over the soft leather. It felt nice.

"Do you have a safe word?"

"No, Sir." Rachel had read about safe words, but hadn't yet got round to thinking of one.

"The club safe word at Boundaries is 'red' so I think it's best you use that for now. If you panic or if something becomes too much, you should use your safe word and everything will stop at once. Do you understand?"

"Yes, Sir." Somehow, talking about safe words was making all this so much more real and Rachel felt a nervous twitch eating away at her stomach. She wondered how Luke would react if she used her safe word before they even arrived at the club.

As if anticipating her thoughts, he added, "Be aware, though, Rachel, the safe word isn't an opportunity for you to control a scene — it's only to be used as an absolute last resort. At the club, if you're in a scene and you call out the club safe word, a DM will come over and check you're okay."

"DM?"

Luke chuckled. "You really are new, aren't you? A DM is a Dungeon Monitor. At Boundaries, they wear red T-shirts with the letters DM in black on both the front and back. They're there to protect you, but will also be happy to offer advice and show you how some of the equipment works."

"Okay. Er, Luke? Is it all right to call you Luke?"

He frowned. "I thought I'd asked you to address me as Sir?"

"Sorry, Sir. I've read there are certain protocols and stuff. Are there any at Boundaries I should be aware of?"

Luke leaned over and kissed her on the lips. "That's a very good question, and yes there are certain rules you need to be aware of. First and most important, *never* interrupt a scene. I can't stress that enough. Apart from that, it's the usual — keep your eyes lowered, never make eye contact with another Dom and don't speak unless you have permission to. The main bar area is more relaxed, though, and it's up to the Dom's personal preference as to what the level of protocol should be."

Rachel listened silently. A part of her felt angry at such ridiculous rules and yet another part of her found it strangely erotic at the same time.

"You should avoid going downstairs to the dungeons," Luke continued. He was stroking her thigh very lightly with his hand, with just enough pressure to make her shiver.

"I don't think I'd want to go down there anyway, they sound a bit scary."

"The downstairs dungeons are definitely for the more experienced. It's the only place in the club where edge play is permitted."

"Edge play?" Even the name made her uncomfortable.

Luke shrugged. "Fire play, knife play, sensory deprivation, things like that. You will see it one day, but not yet. You'll like the upstairs playrooms, though." He smiled, mischievously, tickling her on the inside of her thigh.

"Playrooms? What exactly happens in a playroom?" She could guess the answer, but wanted to hear him tell her about it, so she feigned ignorance.

"It's where all the fun stuff happens. Amongst other things, there are spanking benches, St Andrew's crosses and lots and lots of chains," he teased, playfully.

Wow, spanking benches, she certainly didn't have to ask what those were. She wondered if Luke would be putting her over one tonight, and the thought sent a strong shudder of excitement through her.

Luke obviously noticed and gave her thigh a squeeze. Rachel suddenly remembered the driver and looked up quickly to try and catch him looking at them, but he was still watching the road. She wondered if he'd been listening to everything and if he was planning on sharing his juicy gossip with his mates at the pub later.

"Right, we're nearly there. Are you ready?"

No. I think I've changed my mind. Seeing the lights in the distance drawing nearer made her stomach clench into a tight knot and her heart beat even faster than it had a few minutes ago.

"Rachel. Answer me, are you ready?"

His sharp voice snapped her out of her momentary panic and she nodded. "Yes, Sir."

She looked out of the window as the cab pulled up outside a seemingly disused warehouse in the middle of nowhere. The only indication that there was any sign of life were the bright floodlights above them.

Luke opened the door to the cab and held it for Rachel. "Thanks, Rob," he said, and swung the door closed when Rachel was out.

"Do you know him?" she asked in surprise.

"He's a regular driver for Boundaries," said Luke, with a grin. "Don't worry about what happened in the cab, he's seen much worse than that."

Well, that was at least a small consolation.

Rachel looked up at the shabby-looking warehouse as the cab pulled away and felt a prickle of unease. This certainly wasn't what she had been expecting—an empty warehouse in the middle of nowhere. And she was there with a complete stranger who had cuffed her and could do anything he wanted to her. There was no one around to hear her scream. Suddenly, she wished more than ever that she'd listened to Mandy.

Luke took her arm and marched her toward a large wooden door under a dark canopy. He rang a bell and the door opened letting out the lights, sounds and smells of a busy nightclub. *Thank God.*

Chapter Eight

"Hey, Luke. Good to see you." A giant bouncer shook Luke's hand. He ushered them in before closing the door firmly behind them. Rachel stared around her in amazement. Where the outside of the warehouse had been dark, cold and desolate, the inside was in stark contrast—bright, warm and welcoming. A large reception desk stood in front of a mirrored wall with the words 'Welcome To Boundaries Club' written across it in white neon lighting.

Behind the reception desk, a pretty redhead took their coats and handed Luke a cloakroom ticket. Once Luke had signed them in, the redhead asked Rachel if it was her first time there and when Rachel nodded shyly, the girl welcomed her and said she hoped she enjoyed herself.

Luke then took her arm and led her toward a mirrored door with the words 'Remember—Safe, Sane and Consensual!' written across it. She could hear the muffled sound of music and voices through the door and waited in excited anticipation for Luke to open it and lead her in.

After he'd pushed open the door and gently taken Rachel's arm, she found herself in a very large room with a busy bar running along the length of one wall to the left of them. Ahead were numerous seating alcoves arranged in tiers all around the club, some small and intimate, just right for two people, others big enough to seat around eight. In the middle was a large dance floor that was filled with people moving to the thumping, heavy music. The walls were painted black, and dimly lit wrought iron candle chandeliers hung from the high ceiling. The room had an air of kinky decadence and Rachel felt her body tingling with excitement as she continued looking around.

"Hello, Luke, buddy," said a tall blond-haired man, shaking him by the hand.

"Hello, Harvey. Good to see you."

"And who's this delightful little creature?" Harvey smiled, feasting his eyes on Rachel's cleavage.

Luke laughed. "Hands off, Harvey. As you can see from her collar, she's spoken for."

As Luke pulled her away from Harvey, he leaned down and whispered, "Stay away from him, Rachel, he's a dab hand with a single-tailed whip."

Rachel felt her blood chill as Luke led her farther into the noisy bar, and she tightened her grip on his hand. The room was crowded with people, all in various stages of undress—those who were clothed being mostly in leather, latex or rubber. She almost felt overdressed and was glad she'd chosen the relatively skimpy leather outfit so she didn't stand out too much.

Two men brushed past them, heading toward the bar. The shorter, rounder man was holding onto a leash attached to the collar of the tall, butch man trailing after him. She grinned. *How funny to see the butch guy as the sub.*

She looked around the large room, buzzing with the sound of voices and music. It didn't really look that different from any other club, apart from the sexy attire of the occupants. Mesmerized, Rachel scanned the room, taking in as much as she could. She was fascinated that this place existed specially for people who were into BDSM. People like her! She knew now without a shadow of a doubt that this was what she wanted. She felt at home here with these weird and wonderful kinksters.

As they crossed the room, several people smiled a greeting to Luke as they passed. He stopped for a moment and chatted to a tall, well-endowed woman—a Domme by the look of it. She was wearing black leather trousers with a whip tucked into the waistband and a black leather bra.

Quickly averting her eyes, Rachel continued to scan the

club.

There was a thin film of smoke hanging in the air, although no one seemed to be smoking, but it added to the sexy, intense atmosphere. Then she recognized the smell of dry ice mingled with an earthy smell of leather. And sex! The whole place was heady, sexy as hell, and Rachel felt her stomach flip in excitement. She loved it.

Luke, having finished his chat with the scary Domme, led her past a large, sweeping staircase with tiny little twinkling white lights buried in each step, leading the way up to what she could only imagine must be the playrooms. She smiled to herself and hoped he would take her up there later, but the smile quickly disappeared when they passed another staircase.

This time the steps were going down and looked intimidating and unwelcoming. The stairs at the top were lit, but the farther down she looked, the darker it became, until the stairs disappeared into complete darkness. Heavy chains hung against the black walls leading down the stairs, and Rachel wondered if it would feel a bit like descending into hell if she ever walked down to the dark dungeons.

Thankfully, Luke continued past the 'Stairs to Hell' and over toward the bar. This was better lit than the rest of the room and Rachel was able to catch a glimpse of some of the people standing along it, some on their own, others with subs by their side, clearly identified by their cuffs. They only waited a few seconds before a very tall female bartender approached them. She had the biggest bleached blonde hairdo Rachel had ever seen, backcombed and piled on her head like a bird's nest. The woman had more makeup on than a pantomime dame and was wearing the biggest, most dangly diamante earrings she'd ever seen. "Hello, Luke darling, long time, no see. How are you?" asked the woman in a deep masculine voice.

Luke smiled and pulled Rachel toward him. "I'm good, Chrissie, thanks. This is Rachel. She's a newbie."

Chrissie gave her a warm smile and said, "Welcome,

Rachel, what would you like to drink?" Rachel grinned at Chrissie, instantly warming to the friendly drag queen.

She was about to tell Chrissie what she'd like when she stopped herself. Luke had said she could only talk with his permission, but Chrissie was asking her a question. What should she do? She looked up at Luke for guidance and he smiled at her and gave her a kiss. "Good girl," he whispered into her ear, "you remembered. You may tell Chrissie what you'd like to drink."

Rachel didn't know whether to feel humiliated by Luke's words or happy that she had pleased him. Shit, what was going on inside her head? She'd normally never allow a man to tell her whether she could speak or not, but somehow, in here, with Luke, she realized that she didn't mind.

"I'd like a Coke please," she said, as graciously as she could without looking up to meet Chrissie's gaze.

"Hey, lovey," said Chrissie. "I'm not a Domme so you don't have to worry about stupid protocols with me."

Rachel lifted her eyes and met her gaze. "Thanks," she mouthed, silently.

"How are you feeling?" asked Luke as Chrissie was getting their drinks.

"A bit overwhelmed, Sir," Rachel admitted, hardly daring to lift her eyes to meet his.

Luke took her hand and gave it a squeeze. "Thank you for being honest, that's important here. Just so you know, I think you're doing brilliantly."

"Thank you, Sir." She felt warmth flow through her at his approval. "I do like it here, though. I know it sounds strange, but I feel a bit like I've finally found somewhere I belong."

Luke gave her arm a squeeze and turned back toward the bar as Chrissie approached with their drinks. Luke handed Rachel her Coke, and leaned over toward Chrissie. "Would you keep an eye on Rachel for a minute?"

Chrissie grinned back at him. "It'll be my pleasure, lovey."

Rachel, her brain suddenly comprehending what he'd

said, cried out, "You're not leaving me, are you?"

Luke leaned over and kissed her on the tip of her nose. "I won't be long," he said, then turned and walked off, leaving her alone at the bar with Chrissie beaming at her.

"Don't worry, love," said Chrissie, "you're collared so you won't get bothered, but if you do, I'll look after you."

Rachel smiled shakily at her and looked around for Luke. She couldn't see him anywhere and was beginning to feel slightly uncomfortable. She didn't feel confident enough to be left alone, especially as Harvey kept eyeing her up from a distance. Where the hell was Luke and why had he walked off like that, leaving her alone?

The bar was bustling with people leaning across and pushing her as they tried to get served. Trying to look inconspicuous, she stood silently and listened to snippets of conversation around her.

"It turned out she was a fucking switch!" laughed one guy. "She was about to tie me to the fucking bench and paddle me. Can you believe it?"

"So what did you do?" asked his friend.

"I ordered her to her knees and made her suck my cock before I whipped her arse so she couldn't sit down for a fucking week. She came so hard she begged me to top her again."

Rachel shuddered at the thought and looked desperately around for Luke, and when he still didn't return, her anxiety grew. She picked her glass up and nervously took a large gulp. She decided to distract herself by concentrating on the music, which wasn't quite as loud by the bar. It was some rock group with a female singer. It sounded quite good, actually.

Then suddenly, above the drone of voices and pulsing beat, she heard a voice behind her, a voice she recognized. "Hello, Rachel. Fancy seeing you here!"

Rachel swung around in shock and was stunned to find herself face to face with Adam Stone. She didn't notice the glass fall from her hand and smash onto the floor as everything around her became muted and fuzzy. The background noise faded away and suddenly the only people in the room were Mr Stone and she. Her head was buzzing, she couldn't think straight, other than having an intense awareness that Adam Stone was standing right in front of her.

Slowly, her senses started to return and the fog in her head cleared. She closed her eyes momentarily then reopened them to make sure he really was there. He watched her closely with a hint of a smile on his face, then unexpectedly raised his hand and gently swept a strand of hair away from her face. She couldn't pull away from his gaze, and it was only when someone brushed against her leg as they cleared up the broken glass that the spell was broken.

He looked so different. He wasn't wearing the usual sharp, handmade business suit she was getting used to. Instead he was wearing black leather trousers and a tight-fitting black T-shirt that showed off his muscled torso and strong tattooed arms. He seemed bigger somehow, taller and more rugged, and even more damned gorgeous than ever.

She drew in a breath as she took in his dark, silver-streaked hair, which looked longer now that it wasn't so immaculately styled. It was ruffled and shaggy, but that only made him look even more dangerous and sexy. His blue eyes were just as commanding and sharp as they had been earlier that day when he'd watched her squirm over her unfortunate Internet search. He looked like a mean, hard Dom and her legs almost buckled under her as desire swept through her entire body.

"What are you doing here?" she finally managed to whisper. The people who had been queuing around her a second ago had strangely disappeared farther down the bar and it felt as if they were the only people there.

"I was about to ask you the same question," he said, with a knowing smile.

"I came with a friend," she said, trying to regain some

73

control of her faculties.

"Oh? Who's that then?" asked Mr Stone, his eyes now laughing.

"Luke," she answered, looking around for him. Where the hell had he gotten to? "What about you? What are you doing here?"

"Me?" He laughed. "I own this place."

No way! Bloody hell, she was in a private BDSM club owned by Adam Stone. Could this get any more bizarre? It seemed that it could, because just then Luke returned and shook hands with Mr Stone.

"Adam. Here she is, as requested." Luke grinned, winking at Rachel. "Delivered safe and sound."

"Thanks, Luke, I appreciate your help." Mr Stone slapped Luke on the back and turned to face Rachel with a triumphant smile on his face.

"Believe me" — Luke laughed — "it was an absolute pleasure, and by the way she passed all the taxi tests. She's a true subbie, all right."

That was when the penny dropped. Anger seared through Rachel as she realized she had been well and truly played. "You did this?" she hissed at Adam Stone through gritted teeth. "You bastard!"

Suddenly, the warm feeling of belonging she had felt earlier vanished, leaving her cold and frightened. She was alone in a BDSM nightclub owned by her boss who had used the most devious tactics to lure her there. Shit, how could she have fallen for it? She knew Adam Stone had been up to something with all his underhand remarks, but this? She'd been lied to and manipulated, and she had been stupid and gullible enough to go along with it.

"Rachel, let me explain," said Mr Stone, clearly not seeing what the fuss was all about. He actually had the audacity to look surprised by her reaction.

"Fuck you, Adam Stone," she screamed, and pushed past him and Luke. "And you too, Luke. I *trusted* you!"

She stormed through the bar, pushing the crowd roughly

aside as she desperately made her bid for freedom. She needed to get away from there — away from all those people and, most of all, away from Adam Stone.

She ran toward the main entrance and into the reception area. Shit, Luke had her cloakroom ticket and her purse and keys were in her pockets. Before she had time to think about what to do, Mr Stone came charging through the door, looking like he might like to kill her at that precise moment.

"Get back in there. *Now!*"

If she hadn't been so angry, she might actually have found that sexy, but she was in no mood for his arrogant demands and pushed open the heavy wooden door then ran out into the dark night.

"Rachel!" Mr Stone was coming after her, damn him, but she didn't know what to do or where to run. Panic gripped her — she was alone, without her phone or any money, and she didn't have a clue where she was. Desperate, she started running — she didn't care in which direction, her only goal was to get away from Adam Stone.

After a minute or so, she stopped for a second, trying to get her bearings. She turned and ran toward the car park, but it was so dark she couldn't see where she was going and ran straight into a pair of strong arms that grabbed her and held her tight.

"Get off me," she screamed, kicking her legs out.

"Rachel, for God's sake, don't be so stupid," shouted Mr Stone. "Where exactly are you going to run to? We're miles from anywhere and you don't have any money. Think about it."

Rachel hesitated. He had a point. "Look" — his voice was calmer now — "come back inside and listen to what I've got to say, and if you still want to leave after that, I'll call you a taxi myself. Okay?"

"Okay," she said, meekly, as any remaining fighting spirit drained out of her, leaving her wondering what the hell this was going to lead to.

Chapter Nine

Mr Stone marched Rachel across the car park toward the lights of the club. They made their way back through the reception and into the warm, noisy bar. He nodded at Chrissie to get her another drink, took her arm and led her across the room toward the alcoves.

"Get off me," she snapped, pulling away from him.

Mr Stone made a deep guttural sound, grabbed her hand, then led her to a table set away from the others, with a large 'Reserved' sign on it. A beautiful woman in a black latex catsuit was lounging on the sofa. She raised her eyebrows as they approached.

"New sub, Adam?" she purred, looking Rachel up and down appreciatively.

"Get lost, Dominique," he growled.

She laughed as she stood up and walked over to Rachel. "My, my, you have been a naughty girl to get your Master so riled," she snickered, before walking gracefully away in the highest heels Rachel had ever seen.

"Sit down!" Adam ordered.

"No. I want to go home," said Rachel.

"I said *sit. Down!*" His voice was angry, unforgiving.

Rachel knew when she was overpowered so, pulling her hand out of Mr Stone's grip, she sat down with an angry thud and crossed her arms. He sat down next to her as Chrissie approached with a fresh drink and placed it in front of her with a conspiratorial wink.

"Rachel..." Mr Stone started to talk, but Rachel cut him off.

"You've been manipulating me the whole time, you

fucking control freak," she spat, with more venom than a poisonous snake.

"Yes," he answered, in an annoyingly matter-of-fact voice. He could at least sound like he was sorry.

"Why?" she whispered, defeat finally replacing her anger.

"Because I want you, Rachel." He was sitting so close to her that she could feel the warmth of his body against hers. She shivered slightly, at both his nearness and his words.

"I see, Mr Stone. And now you're going to say that you always get what you want, right?" she snapped.

"Call me Adam. For now," he said, showing no signs of anger at her sarcasm. "And no, I wasn't going to say that."

He suddenly leaned over and took her mouth, hard. He forced his tongue in, tasting her and testing her. He possessed her and she knew at that moment that she would do anything he wanted. He knew it too because he suddenly pulled away, ran a finger gently over her wet lips, and smiled. "Just as I suspected," he murmured. "You want me as much as I want you."

He waited for her to protest and when she remained silent, he spoke again. "The first time I saw you I knew you were a submissive. Even before IT gave me that report on your Internet search," he said.

"Is that why you brought me up to work for you?" she asked, her eyebrows furrowing.

He shook his head. "No. You really were the next in seniority and your work record was good. It was only after I'd requested you work for me that I had you checked out. It was a very pleasant bonus, though," he added, with a grin.

"I don't understand, Mr Stone."

"Adam," he interrupted.

"Adam. If you wanted me and knew I was interested in BDSM, why didn't you just invite me along to your club? Why all the deception?"

"I have to be careful. I don't want to abuse my position and I wanted to be completely sure that you really were a sub. So, I asked a friend, Luke, to check a few of the biggest BDSM social sites to see if you were a member of any of them and, if possible, get talking to you. I initially just wanted to find out what your level of interest was, but once he made contact with you, he emailed me and I couldn't resist asking him to invite you along tonight." He ran his finger gently along the collar around her neck. "Do you like your collar and cuffs?"

"They're yours?"

He nodded and tugged gently on the metal ring at the front of the collar. "Hmm, I wanted to make sure no one gave you any trouble. You look beautiful wearing it." He leaned over and kissed her, gently at first, then harder until Rachel felt her heart hammering so hard that she wondered if it would explode. He pulled away again, leaving her breathless. "One day I might collar you for real," he murmured in her ear, his voice husky. Heat burned in her groin and she felt her insides melt at his words.

Adam smiled as he watched her reaction and pulled her closer to him, so close that their bodies were pressing together. She could smell him, a mixture of soap, musky aftershave and leather, and she instinctively snuggled closer.

Adam lifted his hand and ran it through her hair, then turned her face to him. His icy blue eyes seemed to look right inside her soul. She knew she would never get away with anything, and that gave him a hell of lot of power over her. "Rachel," he said, his smooth, firm Dom voice penetrating deep inside her head. "I know you're a submissive and I also know that you're attracted to me. I'm a Dom and am attracted to you too. Right?"

She nodded, knowing there was nothing she could say to that. He was spot on. His straightforward words made his next ones inevitable. "I want to be your Dom for tonight, Rachel. Do you agree to that?"

"Yes," she breathed, without hesitation.

His eyes hardened. "Yes, what?"

"Yes, Sir, I agree." She was slowly melting, her stomach turning to a crazy jumble of butterflies and somersaults. He'd just said he wanted to be her Dom, well, at least for tonight, but who knew what might happen afterwards. After all, hadn't he just said he wanted to collar her for real one day? A smile played on her lips at the thought.

"Thank you, Rachel. You have no idea how happy that makes me." He kissed her again, lightly at first then with a new urgency that demanded her complete surrender. She gave it, allowing him to take over her mouth and tongue. She felt a happiness she'd never known was possible, a sort of euphoria floating through her blood.

"Now, Rachel, going back to your bookmarked Internet search at work,. I understand you'd like to know what the letters BDSM stand for. Maybe I can help you with that."

Oh God, that damned Internet search again. She silently thanked the computer and replied, "Thank you, Sir."

"Okay, listen carefully." He cupped her chin and tilted her face up to look at him. "'B' is for bondage. To be physically restrained for sexual pleasure." His face was close to hers and she could feel his breath on her as he spoke. "Does the idea of being restrained excite you, Rachel?" he whispered.

She could only nod, the power of speech seeming to have abandoned her. His grip hardened slightly when she didn't say anything. "Answer me."

"Yes it does, Sir," she gasped.

"What about being tethered to my bed, naked and spread-eagled, available for me to do with as I please? Does that excite you, Rachel?" His voice was silky smooth, but the dark, sexual undercurrents brought her out in a sweat.

"Yes, Sir," she managed to reply. This was what she had been dreaming about—her fantasy—and it looked like it might be about to come true. The thought sent another wave of heat to her groin and her heartbeat quickened.

"Hmm, I shall look forward to that." He ran his finger down her neck and over her chest, bringing it to rest just where the leather of her corset began. He gently eased his finger under the seam and stroked the soft skin.

"Next is 'D'," he said, as he continued teasing her breast. He pushed his hand slightly farther under her corset, but he couldn't quite reach her nipple as the garment was so tight.

'Take it off' she wanted to scream, but thankfully Adam continued speaking before she embarrassed herself completely.

"'D' stands for both discipline and dominance. *Discipline*," he whispered directly into her ear, and she jumped slightly at the impact of the word, "involves punishment. How do you feel about that, Rachel? Does the idea of being punished make you wet?"

"Yes, Sir," she whimpered and gasped when she felt his hand move slowly up her legs to rest on her knickers. She heard him moan his approval when he felt how wet she was and she closed her eyes as she waited for his finger to push the thin material aside. But he didn't—he let his finger rest tantalizingly close to her pussy, but without actually touching it. It took all her willpower not to move his hand for him. She had completely lost awareness of her surroundings now, and she neither knew nor cared if anyone was watching.

"Don't be fooled into thinking that a punishment will always be pleasurable. After all, it wouldn't be a punishment if you enjoyed it too much." He chuckled when her body stiffened slightly and waited for her to relax again before he continued.

"'Dominance' is what I shall do with you. I will dominate you, control you and you will obey me at all times. Is that clear?" He pressed his finger a little harder against the material and Rachel shuddered as more arousal took over her body. She didn't even realize she hadn't replied until he said, "Rachel, if you don't answer me straight away, I might have to consider punishing you before we get to the 'S'."

He wasn't joking, she could tell, and, although she was

looking forward to her first spanking, she was only too well aware of his words about a punishment not always being for pleasure.

"Sorry, Sir," she managed to gasp.

"Good girl." He grinned and moved his finger gently over the damp material between her legs. She couldn't suppress a moan of pleasure and he rewarded her with a couple of firmer strokes.

"'S' is for submission and sadism." His voice took on a slightly harder edge now, which brought Rachel out of her cloud of arousal and back to the present. "Submission is what you will do for me. In order to surrender yourself completely you need to trust me unquestionably. You will show your submission by kneeling before me, by addressing me as Sir and by obeying me. I will reward that submission by giving you more pleasure than you've ever experienced in your life."

"Yes, Sir." Rachel smiled.

"Sadism. Now, there's an interesting one. A sadist enjoys inflicting pain on another. I won't deny there isn't a little bit of a sadist in me—I know how to wield a whip and I enjoy it," he said, clearly enjoying the look of shock on Rachel's face. "However, I'm not a hard-core sadist, I don't get off on inflicting extreme pain and I don't usually practice edge play. I will *never* hurt you more than you can take, Rachel, you have my word, okay?"

She nodded, feeling suddenly very apprehensive. Oh, shit! At least he seemed to let her lack of an answer go this time.

"Finally we have the 'M', which, of course, stands for masochism, someone who enjoys having pain inflicted upon them." He moved his head slightly away so he could study her for a moment. "Hmm, I don't think you're a masochist, at least, not a pain slut. I do believe, however, that you might be rather partial to some of my favorite toys, the flogger and the riding crop in particular."

Flogger, oh yeah, that's a whip, isn't it?

Her eyes widened and Adam laughed. "Don't look so terrified, little sub. Remember, we're talking about pleasure. And don't forget, you can always use your safe word."

He moved his finger away from her knickers and stroked the soft skin inside her thigh, sending little electric currents coursing through her body. "Does that answer your question?"

"Yes, thank you," Rachel replied in a small voice, and smiled, until she saw his eyes harden. She quickly remembered to add, "Sir." That was without doubt the sexiest explanation of anything she could ever have imagined. Rachel knew she was hooked.

Adam smiled and gently ran his knuckles over the leather covering Rachel's breasts. "Tell me how you became interested in BDSM," he said, and gave her breast a gentle squeeze.

She felt her cheeks burn as she thought of the least embarrassing way to explain her kinky fantasies. "Well, I... I've been having these dreams," she admitted, shyly.

"Erotic dreams?" he asked, placing emphasis on the word erotic.

"Er, yes, Sir." *Please don't ask what they were about,* she begged silently. She wasn't sure she would survive the embarrassment of admitting to Adam Stone that she'd been dreaming about being spanked.

"What happened in your dreams," he pressed. "Tell me everything."

Oh, God, she wasn't sure she could do this. "I... I..."

"Oh, come on, Rachel," he snapped, "if you can't even tell me about a simple dream, how are you going to cope when I order you to strip and kneel at my feet?"

Adam's words sent little sparks of lust sizzling through her blood, making her skin tingle and her cheeks flush. *Concentrate on the dreams,* she told herself, as images of herself kneeling naked in front of Adam Stone taunted her. He had a point — they were only dreams for God's sake. So she took a deep breath and answered as truthfully as she could. "They all involved BDSM in one way or another. I was always restrained, sometimes blindfolded, and they also always involved being spanked. Oh and the sex was very hot." What the hell, she might as well say it as it was.

Adam grinned. "And, in your dreams, did you enjoy it?"

"Yes, Sir." She cast her eyes downwards and she wished he'd drop the bloody subject now.

"Tell me about your last dream. When was it?"

"Last night, just before I arranged to meet Luke tonight. It woke me up."

"And were you feeling horny and frustrated when you woke?"

God, he was persistent. She couldn't keep the edge out of her voice as she replied, "Yes, Sir."

"Did you masturbate?" He'd said it so simply he might as well have asked if she had cleaned her teeth.

Rachel gaped at him. She couldn't believe he'd just asked her that. "No," she said, the burning in her face now so deep she felt like she was on fire. "I went to check the BDSM site instead and then got distracted when Luke invited me here tonight."

"Just one more question." He leaned over and whispered in her ear. "Who spanked you in your dreams, Rachel? Who was your lover?"

She could tell he already knew the answer so there was no point in making anything up. She took a deep breath and said in a husky voice, "You, Sir."

Adam leaned back with a satisfied smile. "Good girl. You were honest with me and for that I might just reward you by making your dream come true."

Yes please! she wanted to shout, but instead managed a demure, "Thank you, Sir."

"But first, finish your drink because I'm taking you on a tour of the playrooms. You'll be seeing a lot of them in the future so you may as well get acquainted now."

83

Chapter Ten

Adam stood up and held his hand out to Rachel. He was either being a gentleman or he wanted to control her already, she couldn't decide which. He led her to the two staircases near the entrance, stopping briefly to talk to someone at the top of the 'Stairs to Hell'. She could hear loud, heavy music thumping from the darkness and when she heard an anguished scream drift up, the hair on the back of her neck prickled.

Luckily, when he'd finished his short chat, Adam led her past the doomed stairs and toward the welcoming stairs leading up to the playrooms. Her trepidation lifted as the pretty recessed fairy lights on each step led them up to the top, and when Adam pushed a heavy wooden door open she felt a rush of adrenaline shoot through her as the sights, sounds and smells of hot sex greeted her.

Heavy industrial music filled the room, but that didn't hide the moans and cries coming from all directions. Her eyes widened as she scanned the enormous room, which probably stretched the whole length of the large warehouse. Down the middle was a very long and wide space, filled with benches of various shapes and sizes and several plush red leather sofas. Each bench was occupied with a restrained sub, all in various stages of ecstasy, most being spanked with paddles, floggers or whips although one poor guy was getting his arse caned and another was being whipped with a leather strap.

She flinched as she heard the whoosh of the strap tear into the sub's flesh and quickly looked away before Adam saw her staring. *Heaven forbid!* She wouldn't want him thinking she was into that sort of pain.

Along both sides of the center space were lots of little rooms, each partitioned off on either side. There were no walls or screens at the entrance to each room, though, they were completely open so anyone passing could stop and watch the scene taking place inside. There must have been at least twelve, six along each side, plus all the stuff in the middle — wow, this was some playroom! A couple of Dungeon Monitors were chatting amiably to some of the players and, despite the nature of the area, the atmosphere in the room was friendly and relaxed.

Adam led her farther into the room, past crowds of people watching the scenes taking place in the small rooms. Every partitioned room had an audience, but it didn't seem to bother the occupants. The whole place was buzzing with people, noise and sex and it didn't take Rachel long to get caught up in the erotic excitement. It certainly didn't take her long to realize that she wanted to play up there too. She looked up at Adam hopefully and he gave a subtle wink to show he knew what she was thinking.

She hadn't realized at first that the partitioned rooms were themed. It was only when they stopped at a room that looked like an old-fashioned classroom, with a blackboard and a few old wooden desks, that she worked it out. A woman wearing a school uniform, looking a bit like a reject from St Trinian's, was bent over a chair, her knickers around her ankles.

A tall Domme, posing as a teacher, was striding around the girl bent over the chair, tapping a cane against her hand and telling the girl how naughty she had been. She then placed the cane against the backs of the girl's legs and gently tapped. The girl moaned and screamed as the cane came down hard on her, leaving an angry red welt across the back of her thigh.

Rachel stood silently and watched, mesmerized by the scene, trying to imagine what it must be like to feel a cane thrash into her like that. She wasn't sure she'd like to try it, though, and was glad that Adam had said he wasn't into giving too much pain. She looked up into his face and saw him watching her reactions closely.

"Try to imagine yourself in there," he said, his voice soft and husky in her ear. "Now, swap the cane for my hand."

A rush of moisture pooled in her pussy and she unconsciously licked her lips as she imagined Adam spanking her exposed arse.

"You like that idea?" he said, and squeezed her hand. "Good, come on, there's more to see."

Holding tightly onto his hand, she followed him silently. He paused outside the next room, which was bare except for a big cross in the shape of an X against the wall and chains hanging down from the ceiling and across the floor. It looked scary as hell, but at the same time, it was also very sexy.

Adam leaned down and kissed the top of her head. "You'll get to try the St Andrew's cross soon. You'll like it, I promise."

She didn't doubt him for a second and found herself looking forward to being strapped onto the cross, hopefully soon. *Bloody hell, what's happening to me?*

He continued leading her through the wide corridor, pausing slightly at each themed room so she could see what was going on inside. There was a doctor's surgery, an office, a Victorian boudoir, all fully occupied with people acting out their fantasies in their own erotic way. Each room they stopped at, she noticed that Adam watched her closely, as if he were studying her reactions to the various scenes they witnessed.

They continued walking until they came to a room at the very end. Adam stopped and indicated for her to watch what was going on. The room actually looked like a normal bedroom, nothing kinky about it at all. There was a huge bed taking pride of place along the back wall, a couple of chairs and a cupboard, and that was about it. The only difference between that room and a normal bedroom was the open end where anyone could stand and watch the action going on inside.

Inside the room, a sub was kneeling on all fours on the bed while being fucked by two Doms at the same time. One was fucking her from behind, every thrust pushing her forward so she took the cock from the other Dom farther into her mouth with each pounding.

Rachel straightened her shoulders and felt a thin film of perspiration gather just above her lips. There was something very erotic about this scene, but she wasn't sure if it was the fact that the girl was being fucked by two men at the same time, or the fact that they were doing it in full view of a small audience.

Whatever it was, it turned her on, but she certainly wasn't going to let Adam see that, because as much as she enjoyed watching the threesome, there was no way she wanted to do that herself.

"What are you thinking, Rachel?" Adam's voice purred into her ear, making her jump slightly.

"Oh, you know" — she giggled, a little nervously — "I was just wondering what you're going to do to me."

Just throw me across that empty bench over there and spank me hard, please. There's only so much a girl can witness without wanting to join in the fun.

Adam just grinned and took her hand. "So you like the playrooms?"

"You bet," she laughed.

"Good." He was leading her back through the large central area. Every themed room they passed, Rachel wondered if this was the one he would take her to. Or maybe he was waiting for a spanking bench to become free? But he carried on walking toward the door leading back to the stairs.

"Where are we going?" she asked, frowning. She didn't want to go back downstairs, for God's sake — she was so bloody horny now and she wanted some fun.

"Be quiet. You no longer have permission to speak." Adam's voice had changed back to the deep, commanding

Dom's voice. *What the fuck?* She groaned and stomped after him, her shoulders now rigid with frustration and irritation.

He led her silently back downstairs and into the bar, which seemed even busier and noisier than before. They walked halfway back to their table, when he suddenly stopped and turned her toward the tiers of alcoves.

"Look around you, Rachel," he said, softly.

She did and noticed that while they had been upstairs the atmosphere had changed from relaxed and laid-back, to hot and sexually charged. She looked closer at the people occupying the alcoves and saw that quite a lot of the subs were naked and kneeling at their Dom's feet. Wow, something tickled the inside of her stomach as she took in the sexy sight of submission.

Her attention was drawn to one table, where a sub was on the floor being fed by his Master. He had a look of complete devotion on his face and eagerly accepted the food being offered to him.

Her eyes drifted to the next table, where a Domme was fixing nipple clamps onto her whimpering female sub. She felt her own nipples harden and was glad of the leather corset covering her breasts.

Adam took her arm and led her back to their table. As they approached it, though, she heard a scream from the next table and stared in fascination as a young sub was being finger-fucked on the sofa by her macho Dom.

"Is that allowed down here?" she whispered to Adam, still stunned by everything she was seeing.

"Of course." He smiled and stopped by their table. "No intercourse or male ejaculation down here, but apart from that, pretty much anything goes."

"Wow." Her body felt alive with excitement and anticipation and she couldn't wait to find out what Adam planned to do with her. At that moment, he could have done pretty much anything, she was that turned on. Until he sat down and told her to remain standing.

"Remove your corset," he demanded, quietly.

"What? Here?" Rachel was stunned. Oh God, this wasn't what she had been hoping for. It was one thing for all these other subs being naked, but she was new to all this. Surely he wasn't going to make her strip in front of everyone?

"I won't say it again, Rachel. Remove. Your. Corset!" This time his voice wasn't quiet and several people turned around to see what was going on.

Keen not to draw too much attention to herself, she realized she had no option but to comply before he raised his voice even more. Slowly, with shaking hands, she started undoing the lacing she had so painstakingly tightened earlier that evening, until her breasts sprang out of the leather, and the corset dropped to the floor. Shit, her nipples were so hard they might as well have been shouting out 'Hey everyone, look at how turned on this tramp is!'

"Good girl," drawled Adam, with a wicked glint in his eyes. "Now remove your knickers."

Rachel could only stare at him in stunned disbelief. *No, please don't embarrass me any more.*

The cold, angry voice that reached her ears made his intentions perfectly clear. "Rachel, don't turn your first spanking into a punishment because I can assure you that you won't enjoy it. Take your knickers off *now!*"

"Yes, Sir," she whispered, her red face complementing the leather sofas. She decided she might as well get this over with as quickly as possible, so she took a deep breath and quickly started to pull her knickers down her legs.

But, before they even got as far as her knees, Adam held up his hand. "Slowly, Rachel. Don't be in such a rush."

"Bastard," she mumbled under her breath, and glared at him in fury. She tried to slow her movements, but she was so desperate to sit down that she still managed to remove her knickers in less than five seconds. Now the only item of clothing left on her body was the tiny black leather skirt that barely covered her.

"Give them to me."

Her hands were trembling and tears threatened to pool in

her eyes as she handed Adam her knickers. He took them and grinned. "They're damp, Rachel. I'm pleased. You may sit."

She was so cross by the time she sat down, she didn't realize she had an angry scowl frozen onto her face until Adam cupped her chin and lowered his voice in warning. "You have two seconds to redeem yourself by getting down on the floor and kneeling at my feet."

She was about to argue when she heard him say, "One." *Shit*. Just as he said "Two" she threw herself on the floor and knelt as he had instructed. Adam grabbed her hair and tugged gently. "You will remain there until I say otherwise."

At that moment Rachel hated him. Why had she come? If she'd listened to Mandy she would have been saved this humiliation and she would have been able to go into work on Monday morning and face him without any embarrassment or shame. Oh shit, work! How was she ever going to live this down? She closed her eyes and forced back the tears that were closer than ever to spilling down her face. She'd be damned if she'd give him the satisfaction of seeing her cry, though, so she bit them back and tried to think of something else.

After a few minutes of sitting silently at his feet, Rachel's anger had subsided and instead she felt fresh arousal flood through her as she acknowledged the submissive position she was in. Christ, why did she find it such a turn on to submit to someone like this? She wasn't usually like that — in her normal day-to-day life she was an independent, confident woman who would *never* be so fucking obsequious. Was it really worth it just for some kinky sex? She considered standing up, demanding that Adam hand her back her clothes, then walking out with her head held high, but something held her back. Damn him, but she wanted to please him and she knew that by walking out she'd jeopardize any chance of getting that spanking she had dreamt of so many times.

Gradually, the last of her obstinacy trickled away and she

sank slowly back into the role Adam was demanding of her. Hell, if kneeling half naked at a man's feet didn't knock the submissiveness back into her, then nothing would.

She allowed herself a quick glance up at him, even though she was aware that a kneeling sub wasn't meant to look at her Dom unless instructed to. He saw her, and instead of reprimanding her, he gently stroked her hair and smiled.

"You can sit back up now," he said, his voice no longer sounding angry.

"Thank you, Sir," she managed to say as graciously as she could, pulling herself back up onto the sofa. He leaned toward her and kissed her on the mouth, then grabbed her head and pulled her roughly to him, crushing her lips as she gasped for breath. His kiss was hard, rough, demanding, and she loved every second of it.

Eventually he pulled away and ran his finger across her cheek and over her swollen lips. "Are you ready?" he whispered.

She didn't need to ask what for, she just nodded as excitement soared through her body again, reigniting the sparks that had been taunting her earlier.

"Lay yourself across my knee." This time there was no hesitation in obeying and she quickly did as she'd been told, waiting in agonizing anticipation for what was to come. The fact that they were in a room full of people no longer mattered. The only thing that was important now was that Adam was going to bring her fantasies to life.

He slowly lifted her skirt, which he had so kindly allowed her to keep on, and she felt a cool breeze brush against her naked buttocks.

"You have a beautiful arse, sweet thing," he murmured, and gently ran his hands across the soft, pale skin. "I'm going to enjoy turning it a pretty shade of pink."

She felt a shudder run through her body, which headed straight to her pussy, and knew that she was very wet again. *Please get on with it*. She wasn't sure if she could stand the waiting for much longer.

He continued to caress her arse with his hand, teasing her, turning her on even more than she already was then, suddenly, his hand finally left her skin and returned with a loud slap. *Own!* That hurt a lot more than she'd thought it would.

He caressed the burning spot he'd just hit, soothing it gently before hitting her again, even harder than the first time. Her whole body jerked with the impact, pain searing through her and, just as she had dreamed, the pain turned into something else, a feeling of pleasure so intense there was nothing else to compare it to. He hit her again and again, each slap slightly harder than the last.

"Oh!" Rachel groaned, trying to breathe through the pain. This was so much more painful than she had ever imagined, but the pleasure she felt was so much greater as well. Each slap landed somewhere different, spreading the pain. Some hits were light and almost gentle and some were so hard they brought tears to her eyes. After a while, she stopped trying to guess where or how hard the next one was going to be, and just concentrated on the pain and nothing else.

Her whole arse was burning now—every blow felt like it was followed by a lick of hot flame. Still the sensations of pleasure and arousal increased until she thought she would come without him even touching her pussy. Slowly, though, the blows started slowing, becoming lighter until he was tapping his fingers softly over her burning skin, sending new shockwaves to her pussy.

He moved his hand between her legs in search of her pussy and when he felt how wet she was, he moaned his own pleasure. She was lying across his erection and desperately wanted to touch it, to release his cock and feel it inside her. But then he found her clit and that was it, everything exploded and she cried out her release, completely unaware of her surroundings, her body writhing as it spasmed again and again in the most intense and glorious orgasm she had ever had.

Slowly her body came back down from its high and she

slumped in his lap, spent. Adam let her lie there for a couple of minutes before he gently lifted her up into his arms.

"So, did your first spanking live up to your expectations?" he asked softly in her ear.

She looked up into his face and smiled, aware that her eyes were bleary and watery. "Better," she murmured. "So much better."

He smiled and kissed her head. They remained like that for a long time afterwards, she snuggled into him with a dopey smile on her face, and he holding her, protectively. Eventually, though, he lifted her slightly so she could come back down to earth and listen to him.

"Right, Cinderella. It's past midnight and I'm sending you home."

That woke her. "What?" she asked, alarmed. Had she done something wrong?

"I'm taking you to dinner tomorrow evening before bringing you back here. When you get home you will go straight to bed, do you understand?"

Ooh, that lovely deep Dom voice again. "Yes, Sir." She grinned, feeling her stomach clench at his words.

"Rob will take you home." He laughed when he saw her face fall as she recalled her journey with Luke earlier that evening. "Don't worry, he's used to it. Now, make sure you get plenty of sleep because you won't be getting any tomorrow night." Her pussy just woke up again and jumped with joy.

93

Chapter Eleven

"Did you have a nice evening, Miss Porter?"

Rachel looked up at the mirror and saw Rob smiling at her. The driver didn't look like he was sneering at her in a dirty way — he looked respectful and completely unaffected by their earlier journey. Although she'd lost a lot of inhibitions during the evening — after all she'd just been spanked and brought to a climax in front of the whole bloody bar — she blushed nonetheless.

"Er. Yes, thank you." He nodded and returned his gaze to the road.

She sat back and closed her eyes, her mind drifting back to the evening, her nervousness at walking into Boundaries for the first time, her anger when she'd found out about Adam and Luke's deception, Adam's personal explanation of BDSM — wow, that had been so sexy.

She must have drifted off to sleep then because suddenly she heard Rob's voice trying to rouse her. "Miss Porter? We've arrived at your home."

"Oh, that was quick. Thank you." She smiled as he held the door for her.

"I'll pick you up tonight at seven thirty," he said.

"Oh? Sorry, I thought you were one of the drivers from Boundaries?"

He smiled. "I'm Mr Stone's personal driver, Miss."

Why wasn't she surprised? With a grin, she bade him goodnight and let herself in through the front door.

Once she was up on the first floor, she made sure she was as quiet as possible as she let herself into the flat. She didn't want to wake Mandy because she would want to hear every single detail of her night and, although she fully intended to share her experiences with her friend, she was so tired right now that all she wanted to do was sleep.

But she should have known better. "Hey, hon. How did it go?" Mandy was wide awake and was clearly waiting for a blow-by-blow account of her evening.

"Hmm, good," she said, with a dreamy smile. "Tea?"

"I'll make it. You talk," said Mandy. She marched into the kitchen and filled the kettle. "So, what was Luke like?"

"Luke?" *Oh yeah, Luke*. Rachel had forgotten about him.

"Yeah, you know, the guy you were meeting?" Mandy rolled her eyes at her and stuffed teabags into the mugs.

"Oh yeah, he was nice."

"Nice?" Mandy gave her a hard stare. "Just nice? Did he spank you, then?"

Rachel shook her head and grinned. "No, but Adam Stone did!"

"No fucking way," Mandy squealed and stared at Rachel in shock. "You've got a lot of talking to do, girl, so get started."

"It turns out that Adam set the whole thing up. Remember when our computer was broken and I was having all those dreams?"

Mandy nodded and handed Rachel her tea. Walking into the living room, Rachel continued, "Well, I did a couple of Internet searches on BDSM at work and stupidly bookmarked one of the pages because I hadn't finished reading it. Well, after Adam appointed me to fill in for Lucy, he had me checked out and IT gave him a report of my Internet activity."

"So he knew all along that you were into kinky sex?" Mandy was staring at her in disbelief.

Rachel nodded. "Yes, he said he asked his friend, that's Luke, to search all the major UK BDSM social sites for new members, in case I might be on one of them, and get talking to me so he could work out if I really was into it or not. He wanted to be sure."

"Wow, I can't believe he went to all that trouble."

"Nor can I. It turns out that he actually owns the club. He even got his personal driver to pose as a cab driver when Luke picked me up. He had orchestrated the whole thing with military precision." Rachel shook her head as she recalled her fury when she'd found out she had been set up.

"So, what happened? Come on, Rach, I want all the gory details."

Rachel yawned. "Can we talk about this in the morning? I'm really tired and Adam ordered me to go straight to bed when I got home."

"He *ordered* you?" Mandy glared at her in disbelief. "Rachel honey, he can't tell you what to do in your own home."

Rachel laughed. "Of course he can't, silly, I know that. It was just kind of sexy when he said it and I really am very tired." She stood up and stretched. "We'll talk in the morning, I promise. Oh, and he's taking me to dinner tomorrow evening and then back to the club so I won't be around tomorrow night."

She left Mandy sitting, open-mouthed, on the sofa, blew her a quick kiss and quickly escaped to her bedroom. She didn't bother to undress she was so tired, and as she snuggled under the duvet, her last waking thought was of Adam's hand caressing her still-tender bottom.

* * * *

Rachel awoke to the sound of her phone bleeping. She opened her eyes, blinking in the bright sunlight, and wished she'd remembered to shut the curtains the night before. As her eyes adjusted to the brightness, she reached for her phone and squinted at the screen. It was a text from Adam.

Good morning. I hope your arse is still nice and pink! Wear a dress suitable for a smart restaurant tonight. No knickers. Adam x

Her stomach flipped and she laid her head back onto her pillow with a happy smile. Her mind drifted back to last night's events and she wondered what he might have in store for her tonight. She hadn't had that dream last night, but that didn't matter because now she had the real thing.

She glanced at her alarm clock. It was eight o'clock — eleven and a half hours before Rob would pick her up. She closed her eyes and tried to concentrate on what she needed to do today, but images of Adam flashed in front of her and she found herself reliving last night's spanking instead.

She was shocked at how much it had hurt and by how much she had enjoyed it. How could something so painful be so pleasurable? She wondered what it would be like to be hit with a flogger and was rewarded with a surge of heat straight to her pussy.

She briefly considered reaching for her Rabbit, but decided against it. What if Adam asked her if she had masturbated this morning? He would know for sure if she wasn't telling the truth, she was a crap liar.

At half past eight she dragged herself out of bed and tiptoed to the bathroom. Mandy always slept late at weekends if she wasn't working and wouldn't surface for at least another hour, so she had a bit of quiet time. She showered quickly and, just as she was about to put her bathrobe on, checked her bottom in the large bathroom mirror for any marks. But to her disappointment there weren't any. It wasn't even pink. Adam would have to remedy that later, she thought, with a grin.

After making herself a cup of tea, she decided to check her emails and logged on to the computer. The last page she'd visited was the BDSM site and there were a few new messages for her. She skimmed through them until she came across one from Luke, sent early that morning.

Hi Rachel, I just wanted to apologize for my deception. Adam is a good friend and I wanted to help him out, he really likes you, you know. I believe you'll be at the club tonight so I'll see you there. Please don't hate me. L. x

She was just about to type a reply saying that of course she didn't hate him, when she decided against it. Let him stew for a bit.

She smiled to herself and shut the computer down just as Mandy walked into the living room.

"Morning," she croaked, rubbing her eyes. "What are your plans today?"

"We're going to have breakfast while I fill you in on last night and then I'm going to go out and buy a new dress for tonight," said Rachel.

"Okay."

Mandy hated shopping and never volunteered to go with Rachel, which right now she was quite glad about. She fancied spending the day alone, shopping and daydreaming about tonight. She might even see if there was a spare appointment at the hairdressers. Maybe she should get her nails done while she was there?

* * * *

Breakfast with Mandy had been fun. Her friend had grilled her about the night before and Rachel had enjoyed reliving her experience. Mandy, of course, had wanted to know every last detail and Rachel hadn't disappointed. It had been enjoyable and when she'd left to go shopping, she'd had a broad smile on her face as she'd headed off to catch the bus to Oxford Street.

She had shopped until she'd found the perfect dress—deep blue velvet, quite short, fitted at the waist and with a nice plunging neckline. Sexy, but classy. She had then decided that she had another problem. Shoes! She didn't have any that would go with the dress so she had found a gorgeous pair of high stilettos with a deep blue bow that almost matched. A new dress and shoes had needed a nice new handbag to go with them of course, then there had been the cut and blow dry at the hairdressers and the manicure at the nail salon.

Now, two hundred and fifty pounds poorer, Rachel had no regrets as she studied her reflection in the mirror at seven fifteen that evening. She knew she looked good and she felt good too, especially as cool air brushed against her newly shaved pussy. She had read on many different websites that Doms preferred their subs shaved down there, so she'd decided to give it a go while in the bath. It felt very strange, the lack of hair made her much more sensitive to sensation. Even toweling herself dry felt different, but nice.

She'd spent nearly two hours getting ready and had fifteen minutes to kill before Rob came to collect her. She was feeling restless and a little nervous. What was Adam going to do with her tonight? Her stomach fluttered with millions of butterflies in anticipation, but also with a hint of apprehension. What was she getting herself into? With her boss of all people! Would Adam be in the car when it arrived or would Rob take her to some secret venue where Adam would be waiting for her?

She rechecked her makeup for the third time, picked up her new handbag then wandered into the living room to see Mandy. "Will you be okay tonight?"

She felt bad about leaving Mandy alone on a Saturday night. She and her boyfriend of three years had broken up a few weeks ago and, although Mandy insisted it was for the best, Rachel knew her friend was feeling a bit sad. Mandy smiled and said, "Of course I will, silly, don't you worry about me. You look hot by the way."

"Thanks."

"Are you nervous? You look nervous."

"Thanks," Rachel laughed again, not sure if that was a compliment or not.

At precisely seven thirty, a car horn sounded outside. Rob was waiting for her with the rear door open and she smiled her thanks as she slid into the car. "Hello, gorgeous," Adam's beautiful voice greeted her.

"Hi." She suddenly felt awkward. What was she supposed

to say to the guy who had put her over his knee the night before and given her a spanking?

"I trust you slept well?" he asked, seemingly unaware of Rachel's discomfort.

"Yes, very well, thank you," she replied. "Er, Sir."

"Good." He leaned over and kissed her lightly on the lips. "I want to kiss you hard, but I see you've made an effort for me and I don't want to spoil your makeup. At least, not yet. You look beautiful." He trailed his hand over her cheek, down her throat and over her cleavage, generously exposed by the low cut dress. She felt a shiver of excitement as the hot trail his finger left burned into her skin.

"Thank you, Sir."

She moaned slightly as he continued to move his hand down to her legs, his fingers gently brushing the skin over her knees before moving up her thigh. "Let's see if you've followed my instructions," he murmured and moved his finger deftly up to her pussy.

"Hmm," groaned Rachel, as his finger gently teased her. Delicious sensations were rippling through her and, as her heartbeat quickened, she felt the warm, damp evidence of arousal build between her legs.

"Good girl, no knickers. And I see you've shaved for me. I like that." Adam smiled, but much to her disappointment removed his hand. He laughed when he saw the frown crease her brow. "Be patient, sweet thing. All in good time."

"So, where are we going?" asked Rachel, needing to break the intense moment before she made a fool of herself and placed his hand back between her legs.

"You'll see. Do you have any regrets about last night?" he asked, clearly not prepared to let her take control of the conversation.

"No, Sir, none at all. It was…enlightening." A smile played on her lips as she recalled the incredible orgasm he had given her.

"So you're happy to go back to Boundaries tonight?"

Keep talking to me in that voice and I'll be happy to do anything.

"Yes, Sir," she replied a little breathlessly as anticipation surged through her body.

"Good, we can get changed in my office behind the reception when we get there."

"Changed?" Oh shit, she hadn't brought a change of clothes. How could it not have occurred to her to bring something to get changed into for the club?

"Don't worry, I have a nice little outfit waiting for you behind reception." He emphasized the word *little* and she wondered just how little that meant. Judging by the lack of clothing most of the subs had worn last night, she didn't expect it to be much more than a tiny scrap of material.

They drove another fifteen minutes or so until they arrived at London's trendy Mayfair. Rob pulled up outside a small, expensive-looking restaurant and she gasped when she saw the name. The Lighthouse was the most famous and exclusive seafood restaurant, not only in London, but in the whole of the South East of England. It was famous for being impossible to get a table at, and if you were lucky enough to get a booking it would cost you hundreds of pounds for the privilege. The food was reported to be among the best in the world and the three-starred Michelin chef was as famous as the restaurant itself. She silently said a prayer of thanks that she'd gone to the trouble of buying a new outfit.

"Hello, Adam, welcome back," said the maître d', as a man in a black suit held the door open for them. They were ushered to a discreet table near the back, away from the busy main part, but with a clear view over the whole of the restaurant. It had to be the best and most sought after table in the whole place. Secluded, but not excluded.

Rachel sat down as her chair was pulled out for her and a napkin placed on her lap, and before she could even say thank you, two glasses of chilled champagne appeared before them.

Adam picked up his glass and raised it to Rachel, who quickly picked hers up and returned the gesture. "To us," he said softly, looking directly into her eyes and making her stomach flip.

"To us, Sir," she repeated, barely able to catch her breath as his gaze penetrated deep into her and slowly melted her insides.

"You don't have to call me Sir when we're not in a D/s setting," he said, with a warm smile. "Adam will suffice."

"What about at work?" she challenged, with a grin. "Are you still Sir there?"

"Yes, you should continue that. I rather like you calling me Sir at the office."

"Did Lucy call you Sir?" she asked. From what she'd heard about Lucy, she wouldn't have taken kindly to being ordered to address him as Sir.

Adam laughed, a deep throaty sound that sent shivers down her spine. "God no, she'd have been horrified if I'd suggested such a thing."

"So you just made me say it because you knew about my interest in BDSM?" she challenged, keen to learn more about her role at work.

"Yes. I wanted to see how you reacted to it, to see how easy you would find it. You had no problems at all, did you?" His eyes creased and his dimples showed as he smiled at her. Her pulse quickened.

"I was intimidated by you."

"I know, and I still feel bad about the way I treated you on that first day. But don't think that just because we have a relationship outside of work, things will change in the office," he said, firmly. "I can still be a ruthless bastard and will always expect perfection."

Rachel's head was spinning as she processed his words. Did he just say 'relationship'?

"Rachel?" Adam's voice snapped her back to the present.

"Oh, sorry. What did you say?"

"I said, do you have a problem with working for me at the same time as being my sub?" His voice held that Dom tone again, the one that melted her core, and she could only shake her head to confirm that she didn't have a problem with that at all.

"Adam?" she whispered.

"Yes?" He raised an eyebrow and gave her an encouraging smile.

"Last night you said you would be my Dom for the evening. Does this mean that you want to be my Dom all the time?" She held her breath for his answer. She wasn't sure if she should even have asked the question, but she needed to know.

Adam's eyes were warm and his voice soft as he replied, "Yes, Rachel, I'd like that very much. If you agree, of course."

Did she agree? Was chilli hot and ice cold? Too bloody right she agreed. "Yes, Adam," she managed to say, "I'd like that very much."

"Good, then let's drink to that." He held up his glass and they toasted their new relationship. "I must tell you, though, Rachel, that although I don't normally mix business with pleasure, I might just have to discipline you for mistakes in a slightly more interesting way than I would have done with any of my other PAs."

Rachel's smile was so wide it almost hurt. "That's not a very sure way to insure I don't make mistakes. I think I'm going to like being disciplined by you at work."

"Don't be too sure, sweet thing. Your spanking last night was for pleasure—you might not be quite so keen once you've tried it for punishment." His eyes held onto hers, leaving her in no doubt that he meant every word. "I take my role as Dominant very seriously. I can be demanding, unforgiving and will expect your full compliance and obedience. Unconditionally."

Rachel swallowed nervously as realization that this wasn't just a game set in. This was for real. "Yes, Sir," she whispered, "and you will have it."

Chapter Twelve

Adam's eyes crinkled into a smile as a waiter discreetly appeared. Rachel wasn't in the least bit surprised when he ordered their food without consulting her first. She didn't mind, though—she would happily have eaten dog food at that moment, she was so happy.

"So, you're divorced, is that right?" she asked, when the waiter had left again. "I hope you don't mind me asking."

"No, I don't mind. Karen and I finally divorced about six months ago," he said, without looking too distressed about it.

"Why did you split up?" Rachel's curiosity was fully aroused now and she found herself wanting to know everything about this wonderful, fascinating man.

He shrugged. "We both wanted different things," he said quietly. "The split was inevitable, there were no kids involved and she had her work to keep her going."

"Do you still see her?"

"Sometimes. Now, enough about me. I want to hear about you, Rachel. Tell me about yourself."

She sighed and looked away from him for the first time since they'd sat down. Her focus drifted across the restaurant, as she took in the beautiful crystal chandeliers hanging elegantly from a glass roof. The small, intimate tables were generously spaced so no one was too close to anyone else, and were all dressed with crisp white tablecloths, sterling silver cutlery and the finest cut crystal glasses. Small glass lamps filled with red oil threw dancing shadows across each table, the naked flame creating a romantic and intimate ambience.

"Rachel, I asked you to tell me about yourself." His voice suddenly held a hint of irritation and she quickly turned her eyes back to him, but remained silent. She hated talking about herself, about her family, her childhood, her relationships.

"There's not much to tell." She shrugged. "I'm twenty-eight, originally from Basingstoke, single and PA to Adam Stone, my very sexy and demanding boss." She flashed him a grin, hoping to distract him.

Luckily, before he had a chance to push for more information, the waiter brought them their starters — seared scallops in butter and garlic. When the waiter had left them again, Adam glared at her. "You'll pay for that later. You might as well tell me everything there is to know about you now, because I'll get it out of you one way or another. Trust and honesty, Rachel. I expect that from you. Now eat."

"Yes, Sir," she said meekly and picked up her knife and fork. The scallops were delicious and a welcome distraction from Adam's words. He'd said she'd pay for that. Shit, was he going to punish her? She wished she didn't find it so difficult talking about her past. Most people loved talking about themselves, but she wasn't one of them and had mostly got away with it, until now.

As they ate, Adam resumed his quest, changing tack as he said, "You have three A levels, one of them a grade A in mathematics. Why didn't you go to university?"

She looked away again, struggling to meet his eye contact. "I didn't want to go to university. I wanted to work so I could earn money to go out and party. What's so wrong about that?"

"You can party at university," he said, grimly. "Try again."

"Adam, please." She put her fork down and reached over to touch his hand. "You're right, I do have issues, but it upsets me deeply talking about them and I don't want to spoil tonight. I promise, another time I'll tell you everything, but please, Adam, not tonight. Please?" Tears were beginning to well in her eyes and she blinked them quickly away, not wanting him to see her get upset.

She was desperately trying to think of a way to change the subject when, thankfully, the waiter approached with their main course.

As the waiter walked away, Adam stunned her when he asked, "Are you on the contraceptive pill?"

She gawped at him. Well, she had wanted the subject changed.

"Yes, Sir," she said, as quietly as she could. She didn't particularly want the whole restaurant to know the intimate details of her contraceptive methods. Although she hadn't needed it for contraception lately, the pill helped with her painful periods so she'd continued taking it after she had broken up with Paul.

He nodded. "Good. When did you last have sex?"

Bloody hell, he could at least lower his voice a bit.

"About a year ago." Oh God, she really didn't want to talk about this now, but the uncompromising look in his eyes told her she didn't have much choice. "After I broke up with my boyfriend I went off men and haven't dated since."

Adam looked happy with her answer. "According to your records on file the last full health check done as part of your health care package was two months ago. You're fit, healthy and disease-free, right?"

She nodded and shifted uncomfortably. "Yes, Sir."

"Good. My last health check was last week. I haven't had sex since then so I can assure you that I'm also disease-free."

God, she really didn't want to hear this while eating dinner, there's a time and place for all that shit.

"Are you happy with that?"

"Yes, Sir." *So is the whole fucking restaurant.*

"Rachel, why are you scowling?"

"I'm not," she snapped. One look at his face made her change her tone. "I was just hoping nobody could hear you discussing your personal details. *Sir.*"

He laughed, which irritated her even more. "We're practically whispering. You're obviously uncomfortable discussing such important details, but it's necessary in this day and age."

Their conversation for the remainder of the meal was thankfully a lot less personal, discussing their favorite books and films, music and they even touched on philosophy. She had been surprised to find that Adam, although not particularly religious, was quite spiritual and even spoke of having had a paranormal experience when he was younger. She was fascinated by this man and was more than happy to listen to him talk, not only because he was entertaining, but because it meant they weren't talking about her.

When they finished their meal, Adam led her out to the car where Rob was waiting. "I can't wait to get you to the club," he whispered, as the car sped through the dark London streets. "You're in for a real treat."

Rachel laughed. "I can't wait." It was true. She was really excited about going back to the club and more specifically being dominated by Adam again.

When they arrived, Adam led her straight through a door behind the reception into a large, airy office and handed her a piece of shiny black material. He grabbed his leathers, kissed her on the mouth and said, "Put this on."

He headed for the door, turned back to her and smiled, the promise of the delights to come glowing in his eyes. "Meet me in reception when you're ready."

She held up the scrap of material and managed to work out it was some sort of dress, although the word 'dress' was vastly overstated. It was more like a very tight, wet-look vest that only just covered her nipples and stopped halfway down her arse. The front, which was ever so slightly longer than the back, zipped all the way up and just about covered her bare pussy, but the tiniest movement left her exposed for the world to see.

By the time she stepped back into the reception, Adam was back, now dressed in his sexy leathers. He raised his eyebrows and whistled when he saw her. "You look gorgeous," he whispered. He put the collar, wrist and ankle cuffs from the day before back on her. When she was ready, he stood back and looked her up and down with a smile. "Good," he said, and took her arm.

As soon as they stepped into the bar, she felt the same shiver of anticipation she had felt the day before as the music, drone of voices and smell of dry ice and leather hit her. Hmm, she could get used to this. Adam led her to the bar where Chrissie tottered up to them, this time with a bright pink wig on. "Hello, darlings." She fussed with her hair and fluttered her eyelashes as she asked them what they'd like to drink.

"Rachel will have a water," said Adam, without asking her what she wanted.

She glared at him, feeling a fresh surge of irritation. Damn him, she was going to ask for a glass of wine.

"She's had enough alcohol already," he added to Chrissie, who nodded her understanding and told them she'd bring their drinks over. "It's important to remain sober while you play," he said, and led her to the same table they'd had yesterday. The reserved sign was still there, letting everyone know this table was for the boss only.

She slid onto the soft leather seat and looked around the club. It was only half past ten, but the bar was already buzzing with crowds of people catching up with their friends before they went up, or down, to play. The dance floor was nearly full and Doms strode purposefully past with their subs dutifully in tow. The air was charged with sexuality and Rachel felt the now familiar warmth return to her as she looked forward to the night ahead.

Adam then, in full view of the whole bar, lifted what tiny amount of material covered her pussy and started stroking her lightly. She groaned softly as he spread her juices over her clit and gently rubbed.

"Hmm." She closed her eyes and forgot about the crowds.

"Tell me how you feel, Rachel." His voice intruded on

her brain, which had just shut down and only wanted the sensation from between her legs. He grabbed her by her hair firmly with his free hand, pulling her head toward him and finally getting her attention. "I said, tell me how you feel."

"I feel amazing"—she grinned, her voice husky—"I feel sexy and horny and I want you to fuck me, Adam. Please."

"Who?" he growled, with a warning edge to his voice.

Huh, what the hell was his problem? Oh yeah, damn him. "*Sir*," she hissed.

He withdrew his finger, but continued holding onto her hair so she couldn't look away from him. "I think you need a lesson in respecting your Dom," he said, his voice low and dangerous. "It looks like you'll be learning about punishment sooner rather than later."

"Sorry, Sir," she gasped, desperate to feel his finger on her clit again. But he let go of her hair and pulled away from her, his eyes dark and brows furrowed. *Shit!*

Just then, a tall, tough-looking guy wearing one of the black DM T-shirts Luke had told her about approached their table. He coughed awkwardly and said, "Excuse me, Adam, sorry to disturb you, but could I borrow you for a few minutes?"

"Of course. Ask Amelia to come over and sit with Rachel, will you?" He turned to her, took her hands and held them together while he gave her a hard kiss. When he pulled away, she heard a click and realized he had clipped her wrist cuffs together. She was about to protest when he picked up a discreet chain from the base of the seat and cuffed her to it.

"Hey," she said, frowning, "what are you doing?"

Adam leaned over her, ran his hand through her hair before grabbing it again and firmly tugging it backwards, forcing her head back so she had to look up at him. A fresh wave of desire swept through her at the way he so easily commandeered her. "I'll only be gone for a few minutes. Remember the 'B' for bondage? Enjoy it." He grinned and walked off, leaving her chained to her seat, just as a tall, pretty girl with short, white spiky hair approached the table.

"Hi, I'm Amelia." She smiled, seemingly oblivious to the chain securing Rachel's cuffs. She bowed her head respectfully to Adam who nodded at her and turned to leave them.

"Hello, I'd shake your hand, but that bastard has chained me to the fucking seat," Rachel grumbled.

"I heard that," growled Adam, and walked off without looking back.

Amelia burst out laughing and rubbed her hands together. "Ha, it looks like Adam might have got himself a bratty sub."

Rachel couldn't believe Amelia was being so rude. Who the hell was she to call her a brat? When Amelia saw Rachel's expression, though, she quickly said, "Sorry, are you new to this?"

Rachel nodded and Amelia rolled her eyes and said, "That explains it. I wasn't hurling an insult at you just then. A brat is a term used in BDSM for a sub who's a little unruly, opinionated and gives her Master a hard time."

"Oh, I see," said Rachel, not sure if she really did see. Was she unruly and opinionated?

"You've either got to be very brave or an utter brat to call Adam Stone a bastard. Although stupid would also cover it," Amelia said, grinning broadly.

"Oh shit, he's already threatened to punish me," said Rachel, with a worried frown.

"Ooh, lucky you," giggled Amelia.

Just then a huge, thuggish-looking man dressed from head to toe in black leather stormed up to their table. "Amelia?" he growled. "What exactly are you doing?"

"Holy fuck," groaned Amelia under her breath. She practically jumped off the seat and threw herself down at his feet, kneeling before him with her head bowed. "Sorry, Sir. Adam asked me to look after his sub."

Sir made a guttural sound that sounded like it came from a lion, grabbed Amelia by the hair and lowered his head to talk to her. "When he gets back, get your arse down to the dungeon," he growled.

"Yes, Sir," said Amelia, meekly, and remained on her knees until Sir had left. Once he was out of sight, she got up, sat herself back down on the seat next to Rachel and grinned like a cat that had just knocked off the whole of London's supply of cream. "Isn't he lovely?" she drooled, a look of complete adoration in her eyes.

Rachel laughed. Lovely definitely wasn't a word she would use to describe Sir. "Don't you mind him treating you like that?" she asked.

Amelia giggled. "Hell no, I *love* it. It turns me on more than anything. Anyway, I get my own back in the courtroom. I always wipe the floor with him!"

Rachel gaped at Amelia in surprise. "You're a lawyer?"

Amelia nodded. "Yep, we both are, although I'm more senior than he is."

Rachel grinned at the thought of Amelia outranking her scary Dom at work. "He looked pretty pissed off just then. I hope I haven't gotten you into trouble."

Amelia didn't look in the slightest bit worried though and shrugged as she replied, "Nah. He and Adam have an agreement that they help each other out when needed."

"Oh, right."

Amelia nodded her head toward the bar. "It looks like Adam's on his way back over. You'll enjoy being topped by him," she whispered, as he approached them. "See that bulge in his trousers? Well, darling, I've watched a few public scenes he's done here and I can tell you that that's not padding!"

Chapter Thirteen

Rachel dissolved into fits of laughter just as Adam reached their table, his 'bulge' in full view. "Thank you for helping, Amelia. I trust you behaved yourself?"

Amelia looked at Rachel and they both started giggling again. "Yes, Sir," she said, trying to look serious.

"You can go. Your Master is waiting for you in the dungeon."

"Ooh thank you, Sir." Amelia turned back to Rachel and gave her a wink. "See ya, have fun!"

As Amelia scurried away, Adam sat down next to Rachel and pulled her close to him. "What did she say?" he asked, softly.

But Rachel shook her head and smiled. "I can't tell you that. You know, subs honor and all that."

Adam's face darkened, although there was a hint of laughter in his eyes. "Hmm, calling your Dom a bastard, laughing at him and then not answering him when he asks you a question." He slowly unclipped her cuffs from the chain and, leaving her hands clipped together, pulled her up and whispered in her ear, "I think you've just earned your first punishment."

Rachel felt her heartbeat quicken in response to his words.

Adam led Rachel across the dance floor toward the end of the room where the two staircases were. Which staircase would he take her to? Please let it be the one going up to the playrooms. But he stopped at the top of the 'Stairs to Hell' and Rachel felt her stomach drop. She really didn't want to go down there, and held her breath as she waited for Adam to decide where he wanted to go.

"Er, Adam?" she said, nervously, hoping she might be able to influence his decision.

He turned toward her and pulled the ring on her collar, forcing her close to him. "The rules apply now, Rachel," he instructed her. "While we're in the club, you will address me as Sir and you will not speak without permission. Do you understand?"

The jovial tone in his voice a minute ago was gone, and Rachel could see he was in full Dom mode now, and not to be messed with. She didn't even dare answer him as he hadn't given her permission to, so she just nodded and hoped he would be satisfied with that. Thankfully, he nodded back, released her collar and led her to the ascending staircase. She silently said a little prayer of thanks and followed him up.

As they got nearer to the top, though, the sounds changed from the friendly hum of chattering voices to sounds of groans, screams and leather hitting bare skin. Rachel's heart was beating faster now and she grabbed the rail to steady herself as panic gripped her, and she started to hyperventilate. What was he going to do to her?

Adam stopped immediately. "Take a deep breath," he said gently, and held onto her to prevent her from falling.

She did, and after a minute or so, her breathing had returned to normal. "Better?" he asked. When she nodded, he turned and continued to the top of the staircase. When they reached the top, Adam paused by a doorway leading to the playrooms and reached into his pocket.

"Close your eyes," he demanded, and she obeyed immediately. "You've been up here before, I know, but I don't want you to see which room we're going to play in. I want you to use your other senses to tell you what you need to know."

She felt something soft cover her eyes, which was then secured at the back of her head. Adam took hold of her hand, pushed the door open, and Rachel was greeted with the sensual sounds and smells of kinky sex.

She was suddenly very afraid. After all she was being led, blindfolded, into a place where whips, chains and other implements used for torture were the norm. Yesterday, it hadn't seemed so intimidating—she had been able to see what was going on and Adam hadn't talked about punishing her. Right on cue, reinforcing her apprehension, she heard voices to her right.

"Please, Mistress," a deep male voice begged. This was followed by the loud crack of a whip and a groan of ecstasy.

Keep calm, keep calm, she repeated to herself over and over, as she took one small step in front of the other, having only Adam acting as her eyes. Her heart was hammering so hard in her chest that she was finding it hard to breathe, and she swallowed back another wave of panic threatening to engulf her. *Adam won't hurt me,* she tried to reassure herself, until she remembered, yet again, that she was here to be punished.

"Hi, Adam," purred a female to her left. "Nice sub. Where are you headed?"

She heard Adam chuckle and reply, "Flogging room. Want to watch?"

"Absolutely," replied the woman with a laugh. "It's not every day we get to see Adam Stone do a public flogging. Let me call the others over." Rachel heard footsteps click hurriedly away, and choked back a tear.

"Adam?" Her throat muscles were so tight she could barely squeeze the word out.

She felt his strong arms wrap around her and his warm breath on her ear as he hushed her. "Rachel, I won't do anything you won't like. Trust me."

Trust me! How many times had she heard that before? She nodded slowly in response, and Adam gently brushed a tear away that had escaped from under the blindfold.

"That's my girl. I won't leave you alone at any time, I promise."

His words did help to calm her down and, as he started leading her through the room again, she felt herself become more aware of her surroundings. Adam was right—not being able to see where she was or what was going on did heighten her other senses. She could smell the sweat of the players mixed with raw sex, rubber and leather. It was both intimidating and sexy.

Eventually, Adam stopped and positioned her where he wanted her. She heard something that sounded alarmingly like the clatter of chains and felt another wave of fear surge through her body. *Shit, what am I going to do?*

She then heard footsteps walk around her and stop directly in front of her. She swallowed nervously as she waited for his next move. It was so disconcerting not to be able to see what he was up to. He remained silent and still, until she felt a gentle tugging at the zip on the front of her 'dress'. She heard rather than felt the zip being undone, and soon after felt a cool breeze float over her skin. She knew she was naked. She felt vulnerable, exposed, and shivered in anticipation of what was to come.

Then, just to make her feel even more apprehensive, she heard the hushed whispers of a gathering crowd trying to keep as quiet as possible, and felt her face flare up in embarrassment. She couldn't hear everything they were whispering, but she could catch little snippets. "Adam... New sub... Public scene... Nice tits..."

Shit!

She quickly became distracted from the voices again, though, as she felt him lift her hands, still cuffed together, and secure them to the chains above her head. He pushed her feet apart with his foot until she was spread open for all to see, and deftly secured her ankles so she was completely restrained and unable to move.

That was the final straw. Panic set in, and she tugged desperately at the chains, trying to regain some control, until she felt Adam's hands gently caress her back. "Sssh, sweet thing," he whispered in her ear. "This is one punishment I think you'll enjoy. I'm going to see how much you can take so I can push your limits another time, but if it gets too much, use your safe word. Do you understand?"

Even though she was shaking almost uncontrollably, Adam's voice calmed her and she knew he really wouldn't do anything she couldn't cope with. Feeling reassured, she answered, "Yes, Sir," and got a hard kiss in return.

He stepped back, and the crowd that was still gathering around hushed to near silence. Then he started brushing her skin gently with something soft and feathery. It felt wonderful, tickling her and waking dormant nerves across the whole of her body. He ran it over her back, down her bottom cheeks and onto the backs of her legs, before running it back up along the fronts of her legs, lingering momentarily around her mound, before moving up to her stomach and breasts. *Hmm.* She felt her muscles relax as a delicious warmth enveloped her.

Then he moved down to her nipples. They hardened instantly, as the soft feathers caressed and teased them. "Oh!" she moaned in delight when he sucked her right nipple into his mouth. It was hot and wet and he licked and sucked until her nipple started to ache. Then his mouth left again and she felt a gentle pinch, making her gasp as the sensation sent shots of electricity to her groin. He did it all again on the other nipple, and she groaned as she felt herself become more relaxed and aroused.

When both her nipples were burning with pleasure, he stopped and walked back to the table. She heard him put the feathery thing down and pick something else up. Oh God, what was he going to do now? There were a couple of giggles from the audience, which only increased her anxiety. Then she felt something soft and rubbery brush against her skin. It felt like loads of thin strands of lightweight rubber all stroking her at once, as he draped them over her breasts, stomach then round to her back and buttocks.

Hmm, if this is punishment, I'll have to misbehave more often. But then suddenly, the thin strands stopped caressing her and instead came down hard on her arse with a loud slap. *Ouch, that hurt, sort of.* Actually, it was more of a sting and, now that it was settling a bit, it wasn't entirely unpleasant. He hit her arse another six or seven times on the same cheek until it started burning slightly. Thankfully, when it started becoming more painful, he stopped and gently draped the tails over her stinging arse cheek.

She felt herself relax a little until he flogged her other buttock, matching the sting on the other side. Her whole arse was burning now and she breathed a sigh of relief when she heard him walk over to the table and put the flogger down. He soon returned and stroked her arm, lulling her into the false illusion that he had finished.

But when she was relaxed to the point of letting her guard down she felt something rub against the side of her thigh, something cold and leathery, a crop maybe? He rubbed it up to her shoulders and round to the front, over her nipples, then brought it down to her thighs and stopped. The crop lifted off her skin and came down with a whoosh across the crease where her arse and leg joined. *Own!* It felt so different from the flogger, much more intense. She bit her lips as she tried to absorb the blow, then the pain changed, somehow sending pleasure signals straight to her pussy, and she felt her clit begin to throb with arousal so strong it nearly hurt as much as the impact of the crop itself.

He hit her again on the sides and backs of her thighs, again and again, and each time she felt the waves of pain mixed with pleasure caress her, until the sting started to become too intense. But just as she was wondering if she should use her safe word, he stopped and rubbed the end of the crop against her burning flesh. She hung her head as she devoured the sensation, not wanting him to stop, this was the most glorious feeling she had ever experienced.

She hadn't heard him walk over to the table but she did hear him put the crop down. A moment later, she knew he was behind her again, and sighed as his hand gently started caressing her glowing buttocks. Slowly his hand moved in between her legs and rubbed gently over her slit. He moaned when he felt her wetness and Rachel felt her whole body contract as he gently rubbed her clit.

"Oh no you don't." His husky voice made her jump, and she realized he had stopped touching her. "You will come when I say so and not before. I just want to make sure you're enjoying your punishment." He kissed her mouth and moved away again, leaving her shivering slightly as she wondered what he would do next. By now, she had completely forgotten about the crowd and all she could think of were the delicious sensations coursing through her body.

Then she felt it, a flogger, bigger and harder than the first one, probably leather or suede, she couldn't tell, landing with a resounding, heavy thud each time it hit her skin. "Oh God," she cried, as she felt the impacts move along her upper back and shoulders, swinging back and forth, up and down in a continuous rhythm, slowly getting harder and more painful. And yet, with every thud, her pleasure increased, each blow sending waves of passion crashing to her throbbing clit.

Every now and again, her head would jerk up at a particularly hard hit, but apart from that she was beginning to feel as if she were losing control of her movements. But then, as the flogging became more intense, she started to question if she could take any more. The pain, although exquisite, was becoming almost unbearable and she considered again, through the haze in her head, using her safe word. But if she screamed the word out, he would stop and she so desperately wanted him to carry on. So she kept quiet and Adam continued flogging her.

And that's when she finally surrendered to him, the pain—everything. She stopped trying to predict where the next blow would fall, how hard it would be or whether she should use her safe word or not. She let go of the inner fight and, as she did so, her legs buckled under her and her whole world suddenly turned upside down. She was floating, far away, on some sort of cloud. She couldn't hear the crowd or music anymore. Everything became muffled as she allowed herself to be carried away in this strange world where gravity didn't seem to exist.

She vaguely became aware of the chains being loosened and her body being picked up in strong masculine arms and carried somewhere. Then the strangest thing happened— she started laughing, really laughing, so hard that tears were rolling down her cheeks, and she buried her face in the chest of the owner of the arms carrying her. She had no idea why she was laughing so much and the thought that she might be drunk fleetingly crossed her mind.

She felt herself being lowered onto something soft and squidgy then being covered with a blanket while the strong arms continued holding her. Slowly, as she started to come down from her high, she became aware of her surroundings again. She opened her eyes, the blindfold had been removed and Adam was looking down at her with a mixture of tenderness and lust.

"Welcome back," he said, smiling softly as her eyes focused on him.

"Hmm." She smiled, somehow unable to talk. He kissed her forehead and she felt herself slowly drift off to sleep.

When she woke, she felt disorientated and confused. She was still in Adam's arms, and he was stroking her hair. "How long was I asleep for?" she asked, groggily.

"Only about ten minutes," he said, and gently helped her to sit up.

She looked around and frowned. "Where are we?"

"In the aftercare lounge. We're downstairs in the main bar again. It's just through there." He nodded toward a thick red velvet curtain. She looked around the small room, which consisted of nothing but lots of squidgy sofas just like the one they were on. Across the room, another sub was nestled into her Dom.

"I've never felt like that before," she said quietly. "It was incredible."

"And you haven't even come yet." He grinned, leaning down and kissing her softly. "I forgot it was meant to be a

119

punishment once I saw you were drifting into subspace. I wanted to make your first trip a pleasurable and memorable one."

Just then, Amelia's scary-looking Dom pulled the curtain across and strode into the small lounge, carrying Amelia in his arms. He put her tenderly down on a sofa and gently tucked a blanket all around her, leaving her back exposed. Rachel was shocked to see it was covered in lots of angry red welts forming a criss-cross pattern across her shoulders and over her buttocks.

She watched the Dom whispering softly in Amelia's ear and was amazed at how sweet he was being, seeing that he was the scariest, meanest-looking bloke she'd seen in a long time. But then Adam scared her at times and he'd been amazing tonight.

He took a tube of cream out of his pocket and carefully start rubbing it into Amelia's sore skin—Rachel flinched at how much that must hurt. But when she looked at Amelia's face her expression was one of complete euphoria, and Rachel realized that she was just as happy and content as she, herself, had been a few minutes earlier.

She looked up at Adam's face and felt a wave of emotion so intense that it took her breath away. Adam saw her expression and smiled down at her. All was well in the world, until he suddenly said, "Up you get, sweet thing, I haven't finished with you yet."

Chapter Fourteen

"What?" Rachel cried, the mere thought of any more pain bringing tears to her eyes.

But Adam shot her a warning glance and put his finger to his lips. "Shh, this is a quiet area. Be quiet and put this on." He handed her a flimsy black robe, which she took from him with a frown. She gave a sigh of indignation and slid off the comfy warm sofa, wincing as her bottom brushed against the seat. She put on the robe, glaring at Adam as she did so.

It was just long enough to cover her bare, burning arse, but she was glad of it nonetheless, as she pulled the sides together and tied the thin ribbon, acting as a belt. She didn't feel quite as exposed as she would have done without it, although it was so transparent that it left nothing to the imagination.

When she was ready, Adam nodded at her to follow him and she stomped after him into the busy and noisy main bar. He led her to their alcove and helped her slide her bottom along the seat. "How do you feel?" He grinned, wickedly.

"A bit sore, but fine," she said, wishing they could return to the warm intimate space of the aftercare lounge. Her body was still tingling slightly and it was only now that she was becoming aware of the soreness across her back, bottom and legs.

Then a thought suddenly occurred to her. "Do my marks look like Amelia's?" she asked.

Adam laughed and stroked his thumb across her cheek. "No way, sweet thing. I can assure you, they're nothing like Amelia's. Those stripes are from a cane."

"Shit," she gasped. "Amelia's into that?"

He chuckled then replied, "Amelia is a masochist and she has the perfect partner in Jack, who is a sadist. They complement each other very well and genuinely care for each other, although they fight constantly at work. It makes for a very interesting relationship."

Rachel smiled and snuggled into Adam's arms. It felt so right being there, and for the first time in years, she truly felt like she belonged. She felt herself letting go of her inhibitions and just enjoying the moment for what it was. Adam's arms made her feel warm and safe, and she would happily have stayed there forever. She could get used to this.

But then the warning signals started nagging at her, just like they always did when she let her guard down, the ones she always got every time she felt a bit of happiness. She couldn't allow herself to become too comfortable in Adam's arms, she thought, pulling away from him slightly, because he would only hurt her. People always did.

"What's wrong?" Adam frowned, immediately picking up on her change of mood.

"Oh, nothing." She smiled, hoping he'd drop the subject.

But Adam's frown deepened and he lifted her face to his, forcing her to meet his gaze. "Rachel, I'm pretty sure I've already said this, but I'll say it again just in case... The two most important things in a Dom/sub relationship, are trust and honesty. I expect both from you, and you will have mine in return. Now, I'll ask again, what's wrong?" He spoke in that sexy, but scary Dom voice again, demanding and uncompromising.

Rachel felt trapped—this was neither the time nor the place to discuss any trust issues she might have, so she decided that distraction might be the best tactic on this occasion.

"I was just wondering what you're going to do to me next," she said, with a slightly forced grin. "I'm not sure I can take any more pain tonight." That bit was true, and luckily Adam seemed content with her answer as he ran his hand through her hair and tugged at it gently.

"Don't worry, no more pain," he said. "At least not for tonight. But we are going back upstairs where I'm going to give you the biggest orgasm you've ever had in your life."

Rachel felt her body spring back to life as blood rushed through her veins in happy anticipation. "Hmm, can't wait."

"But first, you're going to remove the robe," he said in his deep, stern voice. "Now!"

"Don't be silly," she giggled. "I can't walk around wearing nothing."

Without warning, she felt a sharp sting on the side of her thigh, right where he'd hit her with the riding crop. "Own, what did you do that for?"

"A sub *never* calls her Dom 'silly' and they also never argue when given an order," he growled, looking extremely pissed off. "Now, get on with it. The next words I hear from you should be yes, Sir!"

"But… Yes, Sir," she said, in defeat. She stood up and looked helplessly at the alcoves around them. All were full and she was visible to nearly everyone in the bar. Surely he didn't want her to walk around stark naked, did he?

"Adam," a female voice said, coming to her rescue. Rachel looked up and saw it was the woman in the latex catsuit from yesterday.

But any thoughts Rachel had of rescue were soon dashed, when Adam replied, "Hello, Dominique. This is Rachel. She's about to remove her robe. Would you care to join me and watch?"

Dominique's luscious red lips curled up in delight as she took a seat next to Adam.

He raised his eyebrows and gestured for Rachel to begin. "Go on. Now!"

With her face burning, Rachel unfastened the tie under her breasts and let the robe fall off her shoulders, leaving her completely naked.

Dominique licked her lips and gave Adam's arm a squeeze. "She's quite divine. Are you going to share her?"

Adam growled in response. "No, I just want to remind her that she's a sub and she will do as she's told."

Rachel glared at him, anger washing over her in waves, threatening to spill over into a temper that would only get her into more trouble. She knew now that he was punishing her. He knew she'd been lying before and he was going to make her pay. Damn him!

"And," continued Adam, his voice as icy as his eyes, "she will learn *never* to lie to me again."

Adam stood up and walked over to Rachel, towering over her in an intimidating stance. "Kneel!"

Not in front of all these people, please. She looked imploringly at him, but Adam didn't look in any mood for leniency and pushed her shoulders down, forcing her into a kneeling position.

Oh God, she was kneeling at Adam Stone's feet, completely naked while he towered over her, fully dressed and seriously pissed off, by the sounds of it. She was struggling with her emotions — she should have felt anger and humiliation at his treatment, but somehow, she didn't. Instead her stomach clenched as her body spasmed in a violent shudder of pleasure.

He walked to the side of her, leaned over and grabbed a handful of hair, pulling her head back roughly until she was looking up into his face. A frisson of excitement charged through her and she swallowed as she felt herself surrendering.

"You're my sub, Rachel. Do you understand what that means?" he growled, his voice low and deep, sending shivers through her body.

"Yes, Sir," she cried, breathlessly.

"It means that you're *mine*," he spat. "It means you will obey me. Do you understand, Rachel?"

"Yes, Sir." Her head was spinning as she tried to compute the fierce emotions charging through her. Yes, yes, yes, she was his. Completely.

"It also means you will be honest with me, *always*." His voice remained unrelenting and commanding, melting her insides with each word.

"Yes, Sir." She was aware there were tears in her eyes, but they weren't from anger or sorrow, they were from joy because she finally knew what submission really meant.

"And you will trust me like I trust you," he continued, mercilessly.

"Yes, Sir." At that moment she did trust him. With every last piece of her being, she trusted him, adored him, loved him even.

"You're mine, Rachel." His voice was sending shock waves through her body. Oh, how she loved that voice.

"Yes, Sir, I'm yours. Always." She was nearing that feeling she'd had from the flogging, the one where she had been floating. It all made sense now, she *needed* him to do this to her, to command her, overpower her, control her. This was what it was all about. She smiled into his eyes and he smiled back, the two of them locked in an understanding nobody else could ever comprehend.

He knew she'd gotten it, and gently pulled her back up to her feet and put his arms around her, holding her tight for as long as she needed him to.

After a few moments, he pulled back slightly and looked down at her face. He reached out and gently wiped a remaining tear away and handed her back her robe.

"Thank you, Sir," she whispered, not just for the robe, but for helping her fulfill the need she'd never before understood. She had always known a part of her craved something else, something completely different from anything she had ever experienced, but it was only now that it all made sense. Submission wasn't just about being tied up and spanked. It was so much more—a need, a craving—a bit like an itch that was finally being scratched after years of being unreachable.

Adam helped her slip the robe back on and, without

another word, led her away from Dominique and the alcove toward the stairs to the playrooms. At the top, he paused, kissed her ear and whispered, "No blindfold this time."

They walked slowly across the large, busy central room, past the themed rooms to the sides, before stopping briefly at a room with a St Andrew's cross. The long heavy chains hanging from the rafters and bolted to the floor told her all she needed to know. She glanced up at Adam who gave her arm a squeeze. "I see you recognize this room," he said, softly. "Next time, I'll tie you to the cross. I've got a nice new leather flogger I want to try out and your beautiful soft arse is the perfect target."

A tremor ran through Rachel's body, as she imagined herself strapped to the wooden cross, being whipped with Adam's new leather flogger. Why did that turn her on so much? The suede flogger had really hurt after a while, so she could only imagine what one made of leather might feel like. An intense throbbing between her legs brought a flush to her face and she hastily smoothed down her hair in an attempt not to give too much away.

Adam smiled knowingly and took her arm again to lead her away from the flogging room. Eventually, he brought her to a stop outside a room right at the end. Rachel gasped as she realized it was the room where the threesome had taken place yesterday.

Adam nudged her back and she slowly walked into the room and waited for him to tell her what to do. Butterflies were running amok in her stomach now, and she felt lightheaded with the intense sexual energy charging between them.

He walked over to a chair and sat down, leaving her standing awkwardly in the middle of the room. A small crowd was gathering at the open end — a scene with Adam Stone was obviously quite a draw. She could feel the excitement of the onlookers as they waited for them to begin.

"Take your robe off, Rachel," he demanded, sitting back

casually in the chair and crossing his legs.

She looked anxiously over at the onlookers and pleaded silently with him as she hesitated. Adam just raised his eyebrows and said quietly, "Rachel, the next punishment won't be as pleasurable as the last one." The warning in his voice was clear so she slowly undid the tie and slipped the robe off, letting it fall to the floor around her feet. She heard a few appreciative whispers from the crowd and felt her face burning as she awaited further orders from Adam.

"Now, I want you to kneel down where you are." He watched her obey and when she was on her knees, he smiled. "Good girl. Sit back on your heels, keep your feet together and open your knees."

As she obeyed him, she heard excited sighs from across the room. At the same time, she felt a cool breeze brush against her pussy. She was completely exposed and felt an uneasy mixture of arousal and humiliation, knowing that not only Adam, but also the crowd outside, which was getting bigger, could see the glistening arousal between her legs.

"Now, put your hands behind your back and lower your head," he demanded. When she was in position, Adam stood up and slowly walked around her. His feet were in front of her and she desperately wanted to look up into his face, but she knew that would displease him, so she kept her head lowered.

"Good girl. I want you to remember this position," he said, gently touching the top of her head. "This is what I want you to do when I tell you to present yourself to me. Do you understand?"

"Yes, Sir," she whispered, her voice heavy with submissive lust.

"Good." He glanced over at the crowd and grinned. "Have you ever fantasized about being fucked in front of a crowd, Rachel?"

Even though she had had the odd little fantasy about being watched, she was damned if she was going to admit to it now. "No, of course not..." she started to say, but faltered when she saw the look on Adam's face. Shit, he knew she was lying and she knew that he wouldn't tolerate any more lies from her. "Sometimes, Sir," she said meekly, and flushed when she heard a few chuckles from the crowd.

"Good girl. Well, sweet thing, another fantasy is about to come true. Now, go and lie on the bed. On your back."

She scrambled back onto her feet and walked over to the huge bed, climbed onto it then waited, shame washing over her as she tried to come to terms with being the star attraction in this exhibitionistic floorshow. There was no way she was going to have an orgasm in front of these people, she realized with dismay — she'd never be able to let herself go that much, and knew Adam would be disappointed in her. She closed her eyes and wished the crowd away.

She heard the creaking of leather as he rose from the chair, and her eyes shot open again as he walked toward the bed. He slowly pulled his T-shirt off, revealing his powerful broad chest. The muscles on his tattooed arms flexed as he brought his hands down to his trousers and she watched in awe as he unzipped them and took them off. He wasn't wearing anything underneath and his erection sprang out as the leather descended.

Amelia hadn't been joking about his bulge. He was huge! He grinned when he saw her expression and climbed onto the bed to join her. Slowly, he straddled her and, hovering above her, leaned down and kissed her firmly on the mouth. Sharp shocks of lust charged through her body, straight down to her pussy, and she lifted her arms to pull him down to her.

"Oh no you don't," he said, and grabbed her wrists, deftly clipping her cuffs to hooks in the bed that she hadn't known were there. Maybe this room wasn't as innocent as it had looked.

He sat back and looked at her, arms restrained and nipples rock hard. "Beautiful," he said, softly. Leaning down he covered one nipple with his mouth. She groaned in pleasure as he gently nibbled on the tender nub, and when he released it, he rubbed his coarse thumb across it until it became swollen and engorged.

While he continued rubbing the nipple, he covered the other one and the sensation of soft and wet on one side and coarse and hard on the other made her want to cry out in pleasure. She lifted her legs, desperate to wrap them around him, but was punished with a pinch on her already tender nipple.

Adam sat up, his blue eyes now almost black with lust, and grabbed her ankle. "Naughty girls get their legs restrained too." He grinned, and deftly clipped the cuff to a chain hidden at the bottom corner of the bed.

Once he had restrained her other ankle, exposing her swollen pussy for all to see, he sat back again and watched her wriggle against the restraints. "Remember we talked about you being tethered to a bed and spread-eagled for my pleasure?" he asked, leaning so close to her ear, she could feel his breath. "Well, this is it, baby."

Chapter Fifteen

Adam moved down the bed, kissing her neck, chest, breasts and stomach. Then he moved lower still until he finally got to her pussy. By this time, she was throbbing so much it ached, and she desperately tried to raise her body to meet his tongue as he kissed the soft skin above her slit.

"Lie still," he demanded. "Oh, and by the way, you don't have permission to come until I say you can."

This only made her more desperate and she groaned as he teased her with his tongue, flicking across her slit, pushing through the soft, wet folds until he finally found her clit. Her whole body jerked as he sucked her, and she had tears in her eyes as she tried desperately to hold onto what little self-control she had left. This was just too intense — how the hell was she supposed to control her body enough to stop herself from coming?

She heard someone cough and had a fleeting recollection that she had an audience but, by now, her humiliation and shame had well and truly deserted her, and she whimpered as Adam continued to flick and suck at her clit.

Just as she thought she couldn't hold back any longer, his tongue left her and he sat up again, watching her with fire in his eyes.

"God, you're so beautiful," he moaned.

"Please, Adam," she whimpered, desperate to feel his tongue on her again.

His eyes hardened. "Please, who?"

"Adam... Sir," she finally managed to blurt out and was rewarded with a smoldering smile.

But instead of resuming his delicious onslaught, he got off

the bed and walked over to the cupboard against the wall. "Close your eyes." She watched him pick something up and return to the bed before she closed her eyes as instructed.

Her heart was hammering so hard in her chest, she thought it would explode. What did he have in his hand? Did she dare take a peek? Luckily, that decision was taken away from her as she felt something cold and hard push against the entrance to her pussy. "Ahh..." she cried, in surprise.

"Shush, baby," he murmured, "just lie back and enjoy." She felt him push the dildo farther up and a moment of annoyance crossed her mind—she didn't want a fucking dildo, she wanted him. But then the dildo sprang to life and the most exquisite buzzing started vibrating inside her and she gasped in delight. Then, just to torture her further, his finger started to rub against her clit again.

"You may come now, sweet thing," he said, and tweaked her clit hard enough to make her whimper. That was it— her whole body seemed to explode as fire raged through her from her head to her toes. She screamed as her body was racked, again and again, with the most intense waves of pleasure she had ever experienced.

Finally, the spasms slowed down and her body relaxed as he removed the dildo. She could feel his breath on her face and when she opened her eyes and looked up at his face, she knew he was finally going to fuck her. Even in her sated state, her body was ready for him, and as his thick, solid cock probed her entrance, she desperately wanted to pull him down so he would push fully into her, but the damned restraints stopped her.

As his huge cock slid slowly into her, she remembered the dreams that had started all this. Her dreams were literally coming true. *How cool is that?* That was her final conscious thought, though, because just then he rammed his cock deep inside her causing her to cry out in ecstasy.

He thrust in and out, filling her completely in firm, steady movements. Rachel's body, still aroused from her orgasm a few moments earlier, was responding to his pounding and she felt herself drift off to somewhere else, someplace where pleasure was so intense it took on a force of its own.

She felt him thicken inside her and when he reached down and stroked her clit she screamed at the same time as he exploded inside her. He continued thrusting as her muscles spasmed around his cock until finally he collapsed on top of her, their bodies melding together in heat and sweat.

Eventually, he raised himself and looked down at her. "Wow." He smiled, and kissed her softly on the lips.

"Wow," she agreed, and closed her eyes, glorying in the afterglow of the hottest sex she'd ever had.

"Having an audience didn't seem to bother you too much," he said, with a wicked glint in his eyes, and looked up at the remaining crowd.

"Oh God," she groaned. She'd completely forgotten about them, but now, as reality slowly returned to normal, her whole body burned with humiliation. How could she have let herself go like that in front of a crowd of complete strangers? She thought about her screams as she'd come. Fuck, they'd probably heard her all the way down in the dungeons. She shivered as a feeling of vulnerability washed over her and she suddenly wished they were somewhere else.

"Adam?" she whispered.

"Hmm?" He ran his finger over her hard nipples, sending more aftershocks through her spent body.

"Can we go back to the aftercare room?"

"You really like it in there, don't you?" he asked, with a smile. Then he nodded and added softly, "Of course we can. Can you walk?"

Rachel nearly lied and said no, but she'd learnt her lesson so instead said, "Well, I probably could, but I'd love it if you would carry me."

"Good girl," he said with a grin, "you're learning."

Adam lifted her effortlessly and she snuggled into him, savoring the feel of his strong arms holding her. He carried her downstairs to the aftercare lounge and laid her gently on one of the sofas.

"Hmm," she moaned softly, as she put her head down on his lap.

After a few minutes of drifting in and out of sleep, she opened her eyes when she heard the curtain open, and saw Luke walk in, carrying the pretty redhead from reception. She didn't say anything and just watched as he laid the girl gently down and covered her with a blanket. She smiled at him when he sat down and gave her a wink.

"Am I forgiven?" he asked, in a quiet voice so as not to disturb the peaceful atmosphere.

She looked up at Adam and felt her stomach contract with happiness. She nodded back with a grin and heard Adam say, "I owe you one, Luke."

Eventually, much to her regret, Adam roused her gently and told her it was time to go home.

"What time is it?" she asked, unable to hide a frown.

"Four o'clock in the morning," he answered, then laughed when her eyes widened in surprise. "Your clothes are ready for you and Rob's outside waiting to take you home."

"Oh. Thank you." She suddenly felt deflated – she didn't want the night to end, she wanted to stay with Adam all night, to sleep in his arms and wake up with him in the morning. But she was only his sub, not his girlfriend, and besides, she had to face him on Monday morning. He was, after all, her boss so it was probably best anyway that she left before she got too comfortable in his arms.

She took her clothes and headed for the ladies' so she could get changed in private. How ironic that she should be bothered about getting dressed in front of anyone, when earlier that night she'd been flogged into subspace and fucked to a screaming climax in front of a crowd of complete strangers.

Once she was back in her new blue velvet dress and shoes, she glanced in the mirror to check her appearance. The girl who looked back at her was different from the girl who had entered the club earlier. The dress and shoes might be the same, but the remaining heat on her backside told of a girl who had just had a life changing experience, and it went far deeper than the physical marks on her body.

She had always assumed that her fantasies about being restrained and spanked were purely physical — the fact that she might actually be truly submissive had never occurred to her. And yet, the most poignant and powerful part of the whole night had been the moment Adam had pushed her to her knees, grabbed her hair and forced her into submission.

Her mind and body had melted and, at that moment, pleasing Adam in any way she could was the only thing that had mattered. And yet, she knew that if he asked her to spring clean his house for him, she'd tell him where to stick his cleaning brushes. How could that be? How could she want to surrender to him completely one minute, and yet still remain as fiercely independent as she was and always would be?

She studied her reflection thoughtfully — her hair was a mess, her makeup barely visible except for dark smudges around her eyes, which had that glazed, post-sex look in them. She grinned at her reflection. This was what she must have looked like while Adam had been fucking her and, if that hadn't put him off, he must really like her. Her body tingled as she thought about all the delicious things he'd done to her.

The door from the club suddenly opened and she heard Chrissie's deep voice greet her, "Hello, lovey."

"Hi." She smiled. "Have you finished for tonight?"

She watched as Chrissie sat down on a chair and pulled off her ridiculously high-heeled shoes. "Yes, thank God, I don't think I could have stood for another second in these fucking shoes." She rubbed her feet and grinned at Rachel. "So, did you have a good time tonight?"

Rachel smiled dreamily and nodded. "Oh yes, it was amazing. I don't know how I never knew I was into all this before."

Chrissie laughed. "I know, I was the same. If it wasn't for Adam I'd probably still be well and truly in the closet."

"Adam? Was Adam your Dom?" Rachel couldn't keep the shock from her voice.

Chrissie howled with laughter, her deep voice echoing off the painted pink walls. "Oh, heaven forbid," she choked, wiping tears of laughter from her eyes. "I'm not into the BDSM lifestyle, lovey. But I was a closet tranny for many years and it was Adam who gave me this job so I could be Chrissie the tart at the weekends instead of Christopher the nerd."

Rachel giggled. "You're not a nerd."

"Ask me what I do for a living?" demanded Chrissie, hands dramatically placed on her hips.

"Er, photographer? Singer?"

"Not even close. I'm a particle physicist. Tomorrow morning I fly back out to Switzerland to my job at Cern. I fly back to London whenever I can, and Adam lets me work here so I can 'let my hair down' so to speak."

"Wow, you work at Cern? That's amazing." Rachel didn't know too much about science, but she had heard about the Large Hadron Collider and thought how cool it was to actually know someone who worked there.

"You see? I'm a nerd!" said Chrissie, with a grin. "Outside of these clothes, I'm the most boring, nerdy geek you'll ever meet."

"No way." Rachel laughed. "Chrissie, no matter what you're wearing, dress or suit, you will *never* be boring."

"Well, thank you. So, did Adam treat you all right tonight? I've heard he can be a sadistic bastard."

Rachel swallowed nervously. "Really?"

Chrissie laughed again. "Of course not, silly. I'm winding you up. Did he spank you?"

Rachel blushed as her face stretched into a wide grin.

"Ah, so you've got a nice sore butt now, very pleased to hear it. You know, Adam's renowned for his expertise with a flogger. If you think you're sore now, just you wait."

Chrissie winked at her and laughed when she saw Rachel's horrified face. "Don't you like pain?"

"Erm, well, I'm not sure yet how much pain I can take. This was my first time." Rachel caught Chrissie's eyes in the mirror and grinned. "I'm looking forward to finding out, though."

Chrissie smiled back. "Well, you're in safe hands with Adam. He might be a bad-tempered bastard, but I hear he's a pretty good Dom. Just don't disobey him."

"What do you mean?" Rachel frowned.

"It isn't only flogging that Adam is famous for, he's also notorious for his discipline." Chrissie turned and gave her shoulder a squeeze. "But don't let that put you off."

"Thanks," groaned Rachel, and waved goodbye as Chrissie blew her a kiss and left.

When Rachel emerged from the cloakroom, Adam was waiting for her. "You took your time," he said, frowning. "Are you okay?"

"Yes, thanks. I was just having a chat with Chrissie."

"Hmm, don't go believing everything she says. She may be a drag queen, but she's also a drama queen."

Rachel giggled. "I like her. She's the coolest nerd I've ever met."

Adam laughed and led her through to reception. "I'll walk you to the car," he said then kissed the top of her head.

"Aren't you going home?" she asked, hoping it didn't sound like she was angling for an invitation back to his place, which she was.

He shook his head. "No, I've got paperwork to finish. Now, go home and get some sleep. I don't want a tired PA on Monday morning because I might just have to punish any sloppiness."

Despite Chrissie's words about his reputation for discipline, Rachel raised an eyebrow and said, in her best provocative voice, "Is that a promise, Sir?"

Rob dropped her off outside her flat and waited until

she was inside, before driving off. He had been as polite and discreet as always, and she smiled to herself when she remembered how she had thought he was some random taxi driver who'd struck lucky with a couple of kinky customers.

Mandy—unsurprisingly, seeing as it was nearly five in the morning—was asleep on the sofa, so Rachel covered her with a blanket and tiptoed quietly out of the room.

"Hold it right there!" Mandy's voice was so unexpected that Rachel let out a little squeal of shock.

"I thought you were asleep." She walked back over and sat on the edge of the sofa, nudging Mandy to make her move and give her a bit more room.

"I was, but I heard you close the front door. Okay, Rach, talk. And don't leave anything out." Mandy sounded wide awake now, so any hopes of going to bed any time soon were dashed.

"Well…"

"Go on. Did he spank you?" Mandy certainly wasn't wasting any time in getting to the nitty-gritty.

"He did more than that." Rachel felt the now familiar warmth creep through her body as she thought back to her flogging session earlier. "He blindfolded me, chained me up and beat me with two floggers and a crop." *Ha, take that, Mandy.*

"Oh my God." Mandy was wide-eyed as she looked at Rachel with what appeared to be a new respect. "Did it hurt? Forget I said that, of course it would have hurt." She rolled her eyes and grinned.

"Yes, it did hurt. Not at first, though, he started quite lightly, although I didn't think that at the time. It was like he built it up. It got harder and harder and the more it hurt, the more it turned me on." Rachel shook her head as if hearing herself say the words made it seem quite bizarre.

"Are you still sore?"

Rachel wriggled her arse a bit and yes, it was a little tender, but nothing like she would have expected it to be, so she just shrugged and replied, "A bit, but it feels nice. Warm and sexy."

She stifled a yawn, as the evening suddenly started to catch up with her. Apart from the flogging scene where she had reached this altered state of mind called subspace, she had had the most mind-blowing sex ever, but now her body felt as heavy and tired as her eyelids.

"And what about Adam Stone?" pressed Mandy, seemingly oblivious to Rachel's exhaustion. "What was he like?"

Rachel's eyes blurred slightly as she recalled the way he had gently reassured her before the flogging and had then looked after her so tenderly in the aftercare lounge. And later, when he'd fucked her in front of those people, the look on his face had confirmed that he hadn't been lying when he'd told her she was beautiful. "He was amazing," she sighed, dreamily.

"Rachel, you're looking suspiciously like you might be falling for him. Are you finally letting that steel barrier down?"

Rachel shook her head. "I don't know, Mandy. I really like him, he's unlike anyone I've ever met before and he's brought both my mind and body to new heights I didn't know were possible." She thought back to the look of understanding in his eyes when she had finally acknowledged her submission. It had been the single most powerful emotion she had ever experienced, more powerful even than the feelings of betrayal and bitterness that had haunted her nearly all her life.

Yes, it was very possible that she was falling for him, but that wasn't necessarily a good thing because it meant she would have to learn to trust him. But she knew if she let her guard down and allowed herself to fall in love, she would never recover if, and when, he would eventually leave her, alone, hurt and broken.

She rubbed her eyes to cover the tears that were lurking underneath — another yawn giving her the perfect excuse to drop the subject.

"Sorry, hon, but I need to get to bed. We'll talk tomorrow, promise." She leaned over and gave Mandy a quick kiss on the cheek.

"I'm going round to my parents for Sunday lunch tomorrow, do you fancy coming?" Mandy got up from the sofa and stretched.

"Thanks, but I think I need a mega lie-in and a day of doing absolutely nothing. I'll see you when you get back and we'll have a bottle of wine and a proper chat, okay?"

Mandy nodded, and they headed to their respective bedrooms.

As Rachel slid under her duvet she grabbed the spare pillow next to her and hugged it close. She closed her eyes and saw Adam's face smiling down at her, but just as she drifted off to sleep, the smile was replaced with a look of rejection and the familiar feeling of abandonment filled her as a lone tear slid silently down her cheek.

Chapter Sixteen

Rachel stopped outside the glass entrance to Stone Media and took a deep breath. It was Monday morning and she was about to face her formidable boss who only a couple of nights earlier had had her on her knees, naked and willing to do practically anything for him.

Would he mention anything about the weekend or would he be his usual cold, professional self? Maybe he'd flirt discreetly with her, especially if she flirted with him first. But what if she did flirt and he blanked her? Would he be pleased if she tried to mix a bit of pleasure with business? Or would he be cross and punish her, maybe? Now, there was a thought.

She stepped into the lift and felt her stomach lurch along with it. When it pinged at the top, she stepped out as quietly as she could and practically tiptoed to her office. If she could get herself settled behind her desk with her professional, confident smile in place before she saw him, she could hide behind the illusion of efficiency and follow his lead.

The door to her office was shut. When she pushed it quietly open, she could see that the door into his office was open. Did that mean he was already there? She'd arrived early in the hope that she'd be there first.

"Rachel!" His voice boomed from behind the frosted glass, and she took another deep breath as she flung her coat on the chair by her desk and stepped into his office with her smile fixed in place.

"Good morning, Mr Stone." She melted a little as she looked at him. He looked gorgeous in his dark gray suit and crisp white shirt. He was freshly shaven and a hint of aftershave reached her nostrils, reminding her of his musky scent as he had blindfolded her and chained her up in the flogging room. Heat surged through her body and settled annoyingly in her cheeks, as she fought the overwhelming urge to rush over and kiss him.

"Good morning, Rachel." He nodded at the chair opposite him and she sat down, silently. "Are you comfortable? The chair's not too hard, is it?"

She couldn't stop the grin spreading across her face as she replied, "The chair is fine, Sir."

He lowered his voice. "How are you?"

"Very well, thank you, Sir." *I'd be even better if you'd put me over your knee.* Her eyes watered with shame. *Shit, what's happening to me?*

"Good. I nearly called you yesterday."

"Really?" *I wish you had.* She had hoped he would, and had kept her phone close to her all day.

"I wanted to check you were all right, but I thought you might prefer some time to think, without me bothering you." His voice was soft and velvety and she melted a little more.

"I'm fine," she said, smiling. "You can bother me any time you want."

"Do you have any regrets about Saturday?" he asked, his eyes not leaving hers.

"Mr Stone, let me make something completely clear to you," she said, feeling suddenly empowered by the rather sweet way he was trying to find out how she felt. "You forced me into submission, took away my control and dominated me completely. You beat me with floggers and a crop while I was chained and blindfolded and then later, you tied me to a bed and fucked me hard in front of a crowd."

He nodded, solemnly. "That sounds about right."

"Well, Sir, just so you know, I loved every minute of it and can't wait for you to do it all again." She grinned when

141

she saw the relief in his eyes and couldn't resist adding a little teaser. "In fact, Sir, I was rather hoping you'd put me over your knee this morning." *Shit, did I really just say that?*

"Well, Rachel, I'll have to see what I can do about that. I might just have to punish such insolence." He was smiling broadly now and she felt her insides contract with a feeling so powerful it practically left her breathless. "Unfortunately," he continued, "I've got Joanne Baker — our Finance Director in case you didn't know — scheduled for a meeting in twenty minutes, but don't think you're off the hook."

"No, Sir." She grinned happily and stood up. "Coffee?"

"Yes please." He smiled again and picked up his phone as she turned to leave the office.

"Kneel!" His voice stopped her dead in her tracks, her heart hammering wildly in her chest. Wow, this was *so* sexy. She turned around and practically fell onto her knees in front of him, looking quickly down at the floor the way she knew would please him.

But then she heard him say, "Sorry, Neal, can you just hold a moment." He put his hand over his phone and stared at her in astonishment. "Rachel, what are you doing?"

Rachel had never wished to be swallowed up by the floor as much as she did at that moment. *Shit!* She stared at Adam, her face burning, and stuttered, "Sorry, Sir. I heard you say kneel — I didn't realize you were making a phone call. Sorry." She scrambled up quickly and ran out of his office without looking back.

When she was safely in the kitchen, she hid her head in her hands as embarrassment took over her. *Oh my God, what an idiot.* What must he think? She hurriedly made the coffee, adding milk and sugar without thinking, and had to make some more when she realized her mistake.

When she returned to his office with the coffee, Adam was thankfully still on the phone to Neal. She placed the coffee carefully onto a coaster and hurried out again without looking at him.

A few minutes later, Joanne Baker, the tall, elegant Finance Director, popped her head around Rachel's door. "Is he free?" she asked, her voice laced with educated confidence.

"He's just finishing a phone call," she replied, smiling. "He won't be long."

Joanne looked at her as if contemplating something, and coughed slightly awkwardly. "Rachel, I know you're probably very busy, but is there any way you would be able to help me out?"

"I'll do what I can," she replied, wondering how on earth she could help someone as important as Joanne Baker.

Joanne reached into her briefcase and took out a wad of papers. She held them out to Rachel, who took them and gave them a quick glance. "If you could take a look at these numbers for me and check them over I'd be very grateful. Belinda is snowed under, catching up with everything before her replacement starts, and I'm in meetings all day."

"Okay, I'll do my best," said Rachel, feeling flattered that the Finance Director herself trusted her enough with the figures.

Just then Adam stuck his head out of his office and greeted Joanne with a friendly smile and a handshake.

When Joanne disappeared into Adam's office and she was alone again, Rachel picked up Joanne's papers and took a quick look. She wasn't really intending to start at that moment—after all she had Adam's audio tape from Friday to do—but she soon forgot about that as she lost herself in the numbers.

Forty minutes later, when Joanne came back out of Adam's office, Rachel handed her the papers. "All done. There were a couple of errors, which I've highlighted. Otherwise it's fine."

Joanne looked thrilled. "Thank you so much, Rachel. I won't keep bothering you like this, I promise, but I do appreciate your help."

"You're welcome." Rachel smiled, feeling a buzz of satisfaction she hadn't felt in a long time.

She had always been good with numbers and had found maths easy at school. She had sailed through her maths A level and had seriously considered going to university after she'd left school. Her thoughts darkened as the memories threatened to return and she quickly pushed them to the back of her mind. That was a long time ago—there was no going back now, so there was no use thinking about it.

"Rachel!" Adam's voice broke into her thoughts and she jumped as she snapped out of her gloomy reverie.

"Yes, Mr Stone?" she said, and popped her head around his door.

"Have you finished the report on the tape I gave you on Friday?" He barely looked up as he hunted through his drawer for something.

Oh shit, she hadn't even started it yet. "Er… Not yet," she said, wondering if there was any way she could play for time. Her heart sank when she saw his face darken.

"What do you mean, not yet? What the hell have you been doing all morning?" he snapped, the smile in his eyes now a distant memory.

"Joanne asked me to help her with something while she was in with you." Rachel hated dropping Joanne's name into it, but she didn't want Adam to think she hadn't been doing anything during that meeting. Her head was cast downwards and she looked up through her eyelashes to check if he still looked mad. He did, damn.

"I'm going to see Lord Granville now," he said, coldly. "I'd appreciate it if it's on my desk when I return."

"Yes of course." She could barely bring herself to look at him.

Adam gathered some papers and his phone then walked toward her and stopped when he was in front of her. He towered over her, the dominance that radiated from him reducing her knees to jelly. She struggled to look up into his face without reaching up to kiss him.

He leaned forwards and, for a minute, she thought he was going to kiss her, but instead he whispered in her ear, his warm breath tickling her neck, "I'll deal with you later."

She could only stare after him as he stalked out to the lifts. *What did he mean by that?* She heard the lift ping as it arrived to take him to his meeting, and she jumped as if he'd touched her. She hurried back to her desk and popped on her headphones, but the more she listened to the dulcet tones of his glorious voice, the more she became distracted and made stupid mistakes.

In the end, she flung the headphones off in frustration and stood up and stretched. Her head was all over the place, she just couldn't concentrate on the damned report. What she needed was a coffee, so she made her way into the small kitchen, made herself a drink then returned to her desk.

The office was too bloody quiet. The other two PAs always kept their doors shut and there was no sign of life anywhere. The only sound was the slight hum of the air conditioning and Rachel found herself wishing she was back downstairs in the busy, noisy environment of the second floor. She missed Joe and the girls — they'd always had a friendly chat over their coffee break and she suddenly felt an overwhelming urge to pop down and say hello.

She wouldn't be long, she justified to herself — she could divert her phone to reception and if Adam should come back early she would just say she had needed to visit the bathroom. With a flutter of excitement, she put her coffee down on her desk and made her way to the lifts.

As soon as the lift doors opened onto the second floor, Rachel was greeted with the familiar buzz of phones ringing, printers whirring and people talking and laughing. She looked over toward Joe's office and found a pretty brunette sitting at her desk. She looked happy and confident and laughed when Joe shouted something from inside his office. Everything was carrying on without her, and Rachel felt a pang of self-pity as she quietly observed her old life playing out before her.

Tears pricked her eyes and she quickly pressed the call button on the lift and stepped discreetly back in as soon as the doors opened, before anyone saw her. What had she been thinking? She was on the executive floor now. She wasn't one of the old gang anymore, but one of the 'unreachables' on the top floor. The two just didn't mix. Would things ever be the same when she returned? What if Joe liked the new girl so much that he didn't want her back?

Returning to her desk, she absent-mindedly picked up her lukewarm coffee from her desk and wandered into Adam's office. It wasn't even a week since she had been standing in the same place worrying what Adam Stone would be like, and now, not only was he her boss, but her lover and Dom as well. Wow, what a week! As she stared out of the window, memories of his incredible explanation of BDSM crept back into her mind. A smile stretched across her face as she recalled the touch of his lips on her body, his hands in her hair and his flogger on her arse.

"Enjoying the view again?" He was right behind her. She hadn't heard the telltale ping of the lift and she jumped as his voice startled her.

"Oh, sorry, I was just thinking…" Actually, it was probably best she didn't tell him what she had been thinking.

"Oh, Rachel, what am I going to do with you?" His voice was soft and she could feel the warmth of his breath touch her ears. He kissed her neck and her body shivered involuntarily as he gently turned her around and kissed her on the mouth. His lips were soft at first, but then he took possession of her the way he had at Boundaries and his kiss became harder and more dominating.

The harder he kissed her, the more she melted back into her submissiveness, and she found herself wishing he would order her to strip and kneel before him, so he could overpower her the way he had on Saturday night. But, eventually, he pulled away and tucked a strand of hair behind her ear.

"You're distracting me from my work," he whispered, as he traced her swollen lips with his fingertip. "All I want to do right now is tie you to the desk and fuck you till you scream." His voice was heavy with lust, which intensified the throbbing in her pussy until it became almost unbearable.

"Hmm, yes please," she moaned. Oh, God, what she would give for that right now.

"You're not exactly making it easy for me when you go and throw yourself onto your knees in front of my desk." His eyes creased at the corners as he laughed.

Oh, God. She buried her face in his chest to hide her embarrassment. "Can we forget about that please?" she begged.

"Nope. I intend to remind you of that one for a long time. Come on" — he tapped her bottom lightly — "back to work. Is the report on my desk?"

The report? Oh bugger, the report. The throbbing between her legs vanished and restarted in her head as she recalled the mess she'd made of what little she had done so far. She didn't need to say anything — he could obviously tell by the deep flush on her cheeks — and his eyes narrowed as he leaned toward her. "Rachel, don't think you can slack off just because you're screwing the boss. I've got a lot of work to get through and I need a professional and efficient PA, so you'd better buck your ideas up."

The 'or else' was unspoken but crystal clear. Was he threatening her? Furious, with herself more than him, she nodded. "Yes, Sir. I'm sorry, I'll have it finished before you know it."

"Oh, and Rachel?" His voice halted her as she started to retreat back out to her office.

"Yes, Sir?" She turned back to face him and faltered when she saw the grim expression on his face.

"I'll need you to stay late tonight. I think we need to have a little chat about discipline." He emphasized the word discipline and the promise of punishment hung seductively in the air.

Her stomach somersaulted and her heartbeat quickened as she replied, "Yes, Sir," and turned away from him with an enormous smile on her face.

Chapter Seventeen

At six thirty, Rachel finally finished a second tape Adam had given her earlier that afternoon. She ran her hand through her hair as she went through her mental checklist to make sure she had done everything he had asked. She sent the document to print and glanced uncertainly at his door as the small machine behind her sprang to life.

She'd been rushed off her feet since their encounter that morning and was determined to prove to Adam that she was professional and efficient enough to be his PA. There had been no more fuck-ups or embarrassments, and Adam had been his usual polite and slightly aloof self as she had ushered people in and out of his office. She had arranged meetings, screened calls and made his coffee without any hint that behind the professional facade, their relationship took a dark and kinky turn.

She stood up, smoothed her skirt down and picked up the work from the printer, before walking tentatively to his door. Taking a deep breath, she knocked gently and waited for his response. Maybe he wouldn't hear and she could slip out unnoticed, or maybe he would send her home having forgotten about his earlier threat.

Although she had originally been excited at the idea of Adam punishing her at the office, reality had kicked in as soon as the heat from her arousal had cooled. Apart from the obvious fact that someone could walk in and catch them, there was also the small problem that it might actually hurt. Really hurt. He had made it perfectly clear that punishments weren't for enjoyment and he had looked seriously pissed off with her when he'd hinted at what he had in mind. Suddenly, the idea of staying behind and taking his punishment wasn't quite as sexy as it had been that morning.

She swallowed nervously when she heard his response, and pushed the glass door open with shaking hands. "All done, Sir," she said, smiling with false bravado.

"Good." His voice was steady and his eyes unwavering, giving nothing away as to his intentions. "Sit down, Miss Porter."

Miss Porter? Bloody hell, he hadn't called her that since the first time he'd met her. Was that a bad sign? She sat as instructed, folded her hands on her lap to cover her nerves and waited. He didn't say anything while he read through the report she had just typed, and the silent minutes seemed to drag on forever, increasing her apprehension with every one that passed.

After what felt like an eternity, he eventually stopped reading and raised his deep blue eyes to meet hers, but still he remained silent. Her breath caught in her throat and she uncrossed her legs only to cross them again straight away. *Say something, you bastard.* She felt a rush of blood stain her face as he seemed to challenge her. Finally, she couldn't stand it anymore. "Er, is everything all right?"

He sat back and raised his eyebrows. "You did well with this report, Rachel, but we still need to discuss your performance this morning. Do you remember what we spoke about earlier?" His voice was stern, but there was no anger, thank God.

"You said something about wanting to discuss discipline, Sir." Even as she spoke the words, the warmth from her face shot down to her groin.

"Hmm, yes, *discipline*. What do you think I meant by that, Rachel?" He gave her a cold hard stare and she had nowhere to hide as she fought for her answer.

"Erm, did you mean that you were going to spank me, Sir?" She practically whispered the word 'spank' as her embarrassment quickly turned into arousal.

"Do you think you deserve to be spanked, Rachel?" His voice remained controlled. In fact, everything about him was controlled — unlike her.

She couldn't bring herself to look him at him as she struggled to reply, and lowered her head, almost squeaking when she replied, "Yes, Sir."

"Pardon? Look at me, Rachel, and speak up. Tell me if you think you deserve to be spanked." He sounded more like Adam the Dom now and Rachel felt herself surrender under his ruthless interrogation.

"Yes, Sir, I deserve to be spanked." Her nipples hardened when she heard herself say the words and she knew her arousal was clear to see through her thin blouse.

He stood up and walked silently around the desk to stand next to her. He nodded and she immediately stood up, feeling dwarfed next to his huge frame. He took her arm and led her firmly toward the boardroom. The boardroom? Was he going to spank her in the boardroom? He pushed the door open then led her inside, before closing it firmly behind him.

"What if someone…?"

He put his finger over her lips. "No one but myself or my PA is allowed in here without my permission. We won't be disturbed."

"Oh!" There went that excuse.

"Remove your knickers, Rachel." It wasn't a request.

"But…"

"*Now.*" His voice was uncompromising and she knew there was no point in delaying the inevitable.

The recessed halogen lights were dimmed to the lowest level, making the atmosphere subdued and sultry, and she was grateful for the small amount of modesty the subtle lighting gave her. As she pulled the thin silky material over her knees, she felt a slight chill brush over her bare, sensitive mound, and when her hand accidently touched the gusset, she was shocked at how damp it was.

Adam took the tiny garment from her and smiled when

he too noticed the damp material. "Good. Now, bend over the table."

Oh God, this couldn't be happening. She wanted to run out of the boardroom, out of the building and home to the safe cocoon of her flat, but she wanted to stay even more. Taking a deep breath, she laid herself across the end of the table and felt the cool air tease her buttocks as Adam lifted her skirt and exposed her arse.

She sighed when she felt his hands, strong and hard, caress her. He lightly stroked his fingers up her lower back, across both buttocks and over her thighs, which were now trembling. He was in no hurry and she felt herself relax as she became lost in the erotic massage.

Then, without warning, he lifted his hand and hit her hard on her left cheek, the sharp slap echoing slightly in the still room. Her body jerked, but quickly relaxed again as she took a deep breath. It didn't really hurt that much, certainly no more than it had on Friday night. She braced herself for the next smack at the same time as his hand made contact with her skin again, hitting her in exactly the same place as the first time, only harder. *Own! That hurt.*

Before she had a chance to recover from the shock of the pain, his hand landed hard on the already sore spot on her left arse cheek. Hot, burning pain seared across her bottom as he smacked her again and again, always on the same cheek. Tears stung her eyes as she fought to cope with the overwhelming sensations coursing through her body, and still he continued his ruthless onslaught.

She tried to move out of the line of fire so he would hit at a slightly different angle, in the vain hope that it would offer some relief, but he held her with his free hand on her back, pressing her firmly onto the table, giving her no room for movement.

She kept waiting for her body to absorb the pain the way it had the other night, but she remained painfully aware of every strike. Another hit and she screamed, the agony becoming too much to bear. *Safe word, I need to say my safe word*. Just then, though, a fog enveloped her head allowing her to drift into that wonderful floaty feeling from before. Thank God the endorphins were finally kicking in.

But just as she started to enjoy the sensation, he suddenly stopped and gave her an almighty slap on the other buttock. "Ahh," she screamed, as she crashed out of the euphoria and became aware again of the intense pain on her arse.

Then the bastard started hitting her left buttock again, reigniting the fire that was smoldering on her skin, sparking fresh pain. She needed to escape into that place again. *Go with the pain*. She tried to breathe with each stroke, but every time she edged closer to the altered state she so desperately sought, he would stop and hit her other cheek. *Bastard, he's doing it on purpose.*

"Bastard!" Oh God, did she just say that out loud? A harder strike scorched her raw skin, confirming her fear, and she screamed, the tears running freely down her face now. She no longer cared what he thought—the only thing that mattered was the pain. Oh, the exquisite pain—yes she could feel herself floating again. Then he stopped—again.

"Please don't stop," she cried, "please."

But Adam was having none of it and hit her right arse cheek one final, agonizing time before he gently rubbed the tender skin. He slid his finger down to the crack of her arse and gently probed the ring of muscle around her anus before continuing to her pussy.

She gasped when he slid his finger into her wetness. She was practically dripping and flushed when she heard Adam chuckle and say, "I knew you loved it." Then she heard the sound of a zipper being undone and felt his hard, solid cock teasing her entrance.

She needed him inside her so badly, and it was all she could do not to reach back and pull him into her. "Please, Sir," she begged, "please..."

Finally, with a hard thrust, the dots all joined up as everything made sense. The pain, the torture, all led to this incredible sensation. She had thought she'd hated the pain while he'd been spanking her, but now she realized it had been necessary for her to have this incredible feeling that was taking over her body.

He fucked her hard and had barely started pounding into her when her body arched in an agonizing climax that shook her world. She screamed as she rode the wave of ecstasy, the pain from her stinging arse now inseparable from the pleasure as her body surrendered completely.

Adam continued fucking her through her orgasm, slapping her sore buttocks every now and again sending fresh shock waves of pleasure to her pussy. His cock felt so big she wondered briefly how the hell she managed to take him, but he didn't seem to have any problems as he thrust roughly into her from behind, grabbing her hair and pushing her into the table, emphasizing her submissive stance.

His breathing suddenly increased, coming in short rasps, and he quickly reached down and pinched her clit as she felt him explode inside her. The combination of his pinch and his climax sent her to new heights and she felt her body spasm, yet again, as she screamed out her second orgasm.

Finally, Adam's breathing slowed as he collapsed onto her back. She winced when he brushed against her battered buttocks and smiled as she felt his hot breath in her ear. He started kissing her ever so softly on the back of her neck and, at that moment, she had never been more content.

She was still panting, her breathing shallow and quick, and was still lying limp across the table when Adam eventually pulled himself off her. He stroked her back and gathered her hair in his hand, gently tugging it so her head leaned back.

"By the way, sweet thing," he murmured. "That wasn't a real punishment."

"It wasn't?" *Bloody hell!*

"When I punish you, it won't be with my hand, it'll be with a paddle and it'll hurt, really hurt, so don't try to deliberately provoke me for a repeat of this little funishment."

"Funishment?"

"If this had been a real punishment, sweet thing, you wouldn't have come, and you certainly wouldn't be smiling afterwards. I never intended to punish you properly tonight—I just wanted us both to have a bit of fun."

He lifted her gently up from the table and held her in his arms, careful not to touch her bare bottom. She clung to him, still on a high from the spanking and resulting sex, and breathed in his delicious male scent. Hmm, she'd wanted to do this all day.

"Come for a drink with me," he said, nuzzling her ear.

"Yes."

He raised his eyebrows.

She grinned and added, "Sir."

They found a quiet bar hidden away at the back of Holborn. It was too discreet to attract the tourists and not glamorous enough to draw in the local office workers so it was only half full.

"Glass of wine?" asked Adam, as they approached the bar.

Rachel nodded, surprised that he had actually asked and not chosen for her. When they got their drinks, he nodded toward a free table tucked away in the corner, away from the main bar, and they made their way over. Without thinking, she sat down heavily on the sofa and cried out as her sore bottom took the weight of her body. It took several wriggles and gentle easing onto the seat before she was reasonably comfortable, but even then, there was no escaping the burning reminder of her so called funishment.

Adam sat down next to her and, much to her annoyance, just grinned, clearly enjoying her discomfort. "Is it very sore?"

"Yes, Sir," she hissed, hating him for gloating.

"Good, it's comforting to know I haven't lost my touch." He was sitting so close that his leg touched hers and she instinctively leaned against him, enjoying a new kind of closeness they hadn't shared up until that point. When his hand rested on her thigh she didn't try to move it.

She took a sip of her wine and felt herself relax. "You know, all the times I'd fantasized about being spanked, I never dreamt it would actually hurt so much."

"Well, that is the point," stated Adam, running his hand lightly along her thigh, sending little shivers back to her groin.

"I know, but it's still so different from what I'd expected."

"You liked it, though," he said, telling her rather than asking her.

"What makes you so certain?" She frowned. God, he was so bloody sure of himself.

He laughed. "Rachel, you came so hard you nearly squeezed the life out of my cock."

"Oh yeah. You don't think anyone heard, do you?"

He shook his head confidently. "No, the boardroom is soundproofed for confidentiality and, besides, the door to my office was closed as was the one to yours. Don't worry, our secret is safe."

She leaned across to the table to pick up her glass and felt her body protest as a sharp shot of pain reminded her of her tender bottom. Adam smiled knowingly, but didn't say anything—he didn't need to.

"Have you always been a Dom?" she asked, taking a generous sip of her wine.

Adam nodded, looking thoughtful before he answered, "Yes. Even as I child I was always accused of being a control freak. I always wanted to be in charge—captain of the football team, class rep, even in the Boy Scouts I assumed the role of leader, much to our actual leader's bemusement."

Rachel gave a little snort of laugher. "You were a Boy Scout?" She couldn't stop laughing as a picture formed in her head of Adam as a young boy in a Scout's uniform, telling the leaders how to run the group.

"Don't you dare laugh at me," he said, with humor creasing his eyes. "I'll have you know I was a very good Boy Scout."

"I bet you were a really cute kid. So when did you realize you were more than just a bossy control freak?"

Adam squeezed her knee and slid his hand up her skirt, instantly waking her body up again with a start. "Well, I suppose it was at university. A group of us decided to go camping one night and get drunk around the campfire. There was a girl there, Liz her name was, who I fancied like mad and, to cut a long story short, I ended up tying her to a tree in the middle of the night and told her I'd only release her if she agreed to kiss me."

Rachel, who had been about to take another sip of wine, nearly dropped her glass as laughter ripped through her. That sounded so like the Adam she was getting to know. Just as she was trying to get her giggles under control, he set her off again when he added, "She did!"

"What? Kiss you?"

He nodded. "Yep, and more. That's when I got my first taste of being in control and it just grew from there."

"Have you ever had a vanilla relationship?"

Adam pulled a face. "Yes, it was a disaster. I dated another girl in university for two weeks. I tried, I really tried to do things her way, but she was like a bloody ice cream sundae, full of vanilla ice with lots of sugar-coated sprinkles and fluffy cream. It just didn't turn me on." He shook his head as he thought back.

"What about your wife? Was she a sub?" Rachel wasn't sure if asking about his failed marriage was such a good idea, but her curiosity was fully aroused now, a bit like her body was, and she couldn't stop the barrage of questions bursting to come out.

She soon wished she hadn't asked, though, when Adam's face darkened. He took her chin firmly in his hand and turned her head until she was forced to look into the icy depths of his deep blue eyes. "No, Rachel," he said, his voice husky and dark. "She was my slave."

Chapter Eighteen

"Slave?" Rachel felt the blood drain from her face as she took in what Adam had just said. *Did he really just say his wife had been his slave? Fuck!*

Adam let go of her chin and laughed at her reaction. "I didn't lock her up and force her against her will, you know."

"What exactly did you mean then?" She couldn't stop staring at him in shock, eyes wide and mouth open.

"A Master/slave relationship is similar to a twenty-four-seven Dom/sub relationship. Well, sort of. A slave gives up total control willingly at the moment of collaring, and will submit completely in every aspect of the lifestyle, at all times. A twenty-four-seven submissive will also submit full-time, but there may be exceptions which are agreed at the beginning, although it always extends outside of the bedroom. A sexual submissive only submits in the bedroom. Outside of that the pair are equals. Karen was a sexual submissive, but after we married she told me she needed more and that she wanted to be my slave in a Total Power Exchange. I wanted her to be happy so I agreed."

"So you controlled every aspect of her life?" Rachel was incredulous. How could anyone give up their freedom like that and, more worryingly, how could anyone want their partner to be a slave?

He nodded, studying her closely. "I chose her clothes, what we ate, where she went and with whom when she wasn't at work."

"So you did allow her to work then?" Rachel spat, sarcastically. "How generous of you."

Adam sighed and took her hand. "Like I said, Karen was

157

my sub when we married and it was she who wanted to move our relationship on to the next level. I was happy with the way things were, but it was what she wanted. It worked for a while, but then she started to rebel against my control and it was ultimately that which destroyed our relationship."

"Couldn't you have gone back to a normal D/s relationship when you realized it wasn't working?" Rachel was trying really hard to understand, but she found it uncomfortable and desperately wanted him to say that it was he who hadn't wanted the Total Power Exchange.

But he shook his head. "No, it was too late for that. I think she saw it as an excuse to break free from our relationship. Oddly enough, the split was a relief. I think we both realized that perhaps we'd never loved each other enough to make it work, and accepted that we just couldn't meet each other's needs anymore."

"Do you still see her?"

"Sometimes."

Rachel really didn't want to ask the next question, but she knew she had to know the answer, whether she liked it or not. She didn't want to be presumptuous about their relationship, but they seemed to be getting on pretty well and he did say at the weekend that he wanted to collar her for real one day. Swallowing nervously, she asked, "Adam, are you looking for another slave?"

"Why, are you offering?" he asked, raising his eyebrows.

She nearly choked on her drink and stared at him in shock. Before she could think of any kind of answer to that, he spoke again. "I'll accept nothing short of your complete submission," he said, with a smile playing on his lips. "Come to think of it, I think I'd rather enjoy having you as my slave."

What? Fuck, she wished she hadn't asked now. He must have seen her dismay because he took her head in both his hands and looked at her with his stern Dom eyes.

"Rachel, I don't know where we're going with this

relationship yet, but I do know that I like you. A lot. And I also know you feel the same way, so let's just take this one day at a time and enjoy it. If and when the time comes for something more serious and permanent, we'll discuss it then. Okay?"

She nodded. "Okay."

The thought that this might develop into something more serious scared her shitless. She adored Adam and didn't doubt for a moment that her feelings for him would grow deeper, but that meant addressing issues she didn't want to face. Like trust, for one. She remembered his words about trust in a D/s relationship and felt her stomach tighten into a hard knot. Every time she had trusted someone, they'd let her down, leaving her drowning in a pool of betrayal and guilt. But Adam was right, it was early days and they should just take it slowly and enjoy themselves.

Without realizing it, she frowned. How the hell did someone like him even consider having a relationship with someone like her? He'd soon get tired of her and dump her, so the future of their relationship was irrelevant anyway.

"What are you thinking about, sweet thing?" Adam's voice broke into her thoughts and she refocused her eyes, pushed the dark thoughts from her mind and smiled.

"I was just wondering what on earth you see in me, to be honest. I'm not beautiful or glamorous or particularly clever and you're... Well, you're Adam Stone."

His eyes narrowed, and for a minute she thought he was actually going to smack her. "Don't ever let me hear you say that again. Rachel, you're gorgeous, inside and out, and I happen to know you're far more intelligent than you give yourself credit for." His eyes flashed with anger and he grabbed her wrist and pulled her close. "If I hear you put yourself down like that again, I'll take the paddle to your arse so hard you won't be able to sit down for a week. Do you understand?" The threat in his voice sent a chill through her that settled unnervingly in her groin.

"Yes, Sir," she whispered, melting under his dominance.

How did he do that to her? God, if anyone else dared talk to her like that, she'd be mad as hell, and yet she practically lay down at his feet like a bloody lapdog when it came from him.

He released her hand and the warmth returned to his eyes. "Are you free this weekend?"

A little flip in her stomach made her catch her breath and she knew that even if she had been planning on having tea with the Queen she'd have canceled everything to be free for Adam that weekend.

"Yes, Sir." She tried not to sound too keen, but she couldn't stop that stupid grin from stretching across her face.

"Good." He returned his hand to her thigh and crept it up under her skirt, stroking her very lightly. "I have something special planned for you at Boundaries on Friday, and after that you'll come home with me. Bring an overnight bag, but don't put too many clothes in—you won't need much."

"Yes, Sir," she said, breathlessly. Her heart was hammering hard as she tried to contain her excitement at going home with him after the club on Friday.

"Will you have dinner with me tomorrow night?" he asked, running his finger softly up her thigh again.

"I'd love to." She smiled, attempting to look casual, although his teasing touch was making it bloody hard to keep a straight face.

Adam removed his hand, stood up and pulled her up into his arms. "Good. Rob will pick you up at seven thirty sharp. I won't be around much tomorrow." He raised his eyebrows at her in mock admonishment. "Which I'm sure you'll be aware of if you've checked the diary."

Rachel laughed. "Yes, Mr Stone, I'm fully aware of your comings and goings."

"Good. By the way, you've made quite an impression on our Finance Director."

"Really?" She couldn't think why.

"She said the errors you pointed out this morning were very difficult to spot and only someone with an excellent head for numbers would have picked up on them. Well done, I knew you were a clever little thing."

Rachel was thrilled. Joanne Baker was known for being nearly as hard to please as the great boss himself, and she felt a warm sense of pride at Adam's praise, although she wasn't so sure about being called a 'little thing'.

He took her arm and led her out of the bar. She stepped out into the chilly evening and decided that she would quite like to walk home. It might help her to cool down after Adam's teasing hands had left her feeling horny as hell.

Rob was waiting by the car and she wondered how the hell he knew where they had been. "Hop in, I'll drop you off," said Adam, leading her toward the car.

"Oh, that's okay, I can walk."

"Get in," he snapped.

"You're so bossy," she grumbled, but got into the car anyway.

"Yes, so get used to it." As the car pulled away, Adam turned on the little light in the ceiling of the vehicle and leaned toward her. She thought at first he was going to kiss her, until she felt his breath on her ear whisper. "Take your knickers off."

Oh God, she was so horny, but in the car? She stared at him, half expecting him to laugh and say he was only joking, but one look at his stern, dark eyes told her that he definitely wasn't. *I suppose I should be getting used to this by now.*

She hesitated and looked nervously at the windows. "They're tinted," said Adam, obviously anticipating any excuses she might make. Adam was clearly not going to take no for an answer, so with as much grace as she could muster she wriggled, managing to pull her knickers down below her knees, and slipped them off as discreetly as she could.

Adam reached out and took them from her. "I'll take those. Oh, and for future reference, you are banned from wearing the damned things unless I specify otherwise."

"What? Even in the office?"

He grinned wickedly. "Especially in the office."

He leaned over her and took her mouth, hard and possessively. His kiss was brutal as he forced his tongue into her mouth and demanded her surrender. Her body flooded with delicious, tingling arousal and she kissed him back with complete abandon. When he ran his hand up the inside of her thigh and up to her pussy, she groaned as her muscles clenched with anticipation.

Eventually, he pulled away, leaving his hand stroking her naked mound. "Is your arse still sore?"

Rachel could barely manage to get the words out as she struggled to answer him. "Not really, Sir."

"Really? I'll have to remedy that."

Oh shit, why did I just say that? It wasn't another spanking that bothered her so much as the possibility that he might do it here, in front of Rob. The memory of Luke making her masturbate in the car told her that she shouldn't be too shocked by the idea of being spanked in front of the driver. But still. Adam pulled his hand away and sat back. "Over my knee."

Absolute horror took over Rachel's mind. He couldn't be serious, could he? "Adam, please, not here," she pleaded.

"I won't say it again. Get over my knee, *now!*"

With her face burning with humiliation, but her clit throbbing traitorously with excitement, she turned her body, climbed to a kneeling position on the seat next to Adam then lay across his lap. He moved his left hand up her back, pushing her down so she couldn't move, and with his other hand he pulled her skirt up to her waist and gently rubbed the slightly tender flesh.

"Hmm, still a little bit pink, it won't take much to get it glowing again." Then without further warning, his hand came down hard on her right buttock and she squealed with the shock of the impact.

"Oh God," she cried, as her clit ached with delight at the

fresh sensations blistering her arse. He hit her again and again, reigniting the embers that had been slowly dying on the skin of her buttocks and it didn't take long for her body to tense up as a powerful orgasm began to build inside her.

"Please, Sir, may I come?" she begged, as her body started shuddering.

"Yes, sweet thing, come now." Adam's deep voice was all it took to send her over the edge as wave after wave of pure unadulterated bliss tore through her. Her arse was burning again, but that only added to the intense pleasure as another wave crashed through her body.

Finally, her body relaxed, sated and spent. She gradually became aware of Adam gently stroking her burning skin and the soft purr of an engine reminded her of the fact that she had just succumbed in the back of Adam's car with Rob, if not watching, then certainly hearing everything. She buried her head in her hands with shame. "Oh God," she groaned. How could she ever face him again?

Adam gently lifted her and watched her shift painfully as she tried to sit back down onto the soft leather seat. "I'll ask again. Is your arse still sore?" His eyes were laughing and she could tell that he was just waiting for the slightest excuse to do it all over again.

"Yes, Sir, it's very sore." Her words were breathless as she fought to regain some equilibrium after losing control so completely.

"Good." He kissed her again, this time softly, and she melted into his arms as contentment replaced the urgent desire from a few moments ago. "You're home. I hope you enjoyed your ride."

"It sure beats the Tube." She grinned happily and kissed him again.

"See you tomorrow." Adam playfully slapped her arse as she slid past him to step out of the car. Rob was holding the door open for her and nodded politely when she thanked him. Her face flushed again and she hurried up the steps to the front door to hide from her embarrassment. Rob waited until she was inside before driving off, and as she made her way upstairs to the flat she grinned as she imagined her face to be as red as her newly spanked bottom.

As she got ready for bed that night, Rachel's head swam with excitement and fear. Her dreams had come true, beyond her wildest dreams, and yet there was something about Adam that scared her. Not him personally, she knew he'd never harm her. No, this was something deeper. He expected a level of trust from her that she wasn't sure she was capable of giving.

But it was more than that. Why did she get the feeling that she was heading into something that was way beyond her inexperienced limits?

'*She was my slave.*' Adam's words reverberated in her head. She remembered she'd been shocked, really shocked when he'd told her that. And she'd asked him if he was looking for another slave. His answer had shaken her to the core, something about accepting nothing short of her complete submission.

"Oh, my God," she cried out in dismay. She sat down on her bed with a heavy thump and shook her head in disbelief. Adam stone wanted her to be his slave.

Despite the fact that she liked him more than she cared to admit, did she like him enough to give up her freedom for him? With a sinking feeling deep in her heart, she reluctantly acknowledged to herself that she wasn't sure she would be prepared to do that. Even for Adam Stone.

KATY SWANN

BOUNDARIES

Should Rachel stand her ground and tell Adam that she won't be his slave?

TO LOVE & TRUST

To Love and Trust

Excerpt

Chapter One

Rachel Porter took one final look in the mirror and smiled. She was going to dinner with Adam Stone tonight, and she hoped that dinner wasn't going to be the only thing on the menu.

The night before, she'd been on the verge of ringing him and telling him she didn't want to see him anymore. His revelation that his ex-wife had been his slave had stunned her, and when he'd then hinted that he might expect the same from her, she had panicked. But this morning, she had thought about it rationally and decided that she must have heard wrong. She had quickly buried her misgivings and had focused all her energy on tonight.

She returned her gaze to the mirror. For once she was happy with the image staring back at her. Her eyes had a sparkle in them that hadn't been there before—they seemed greener somehow, more like emeralds instead of the usual dull moss-green. Her lips were fuller. In fact, when she really looked, she could almost see a rosy pout where before, her lips had been tense and drawn together. And her hair, looked different too, somehow shinier and sleeker as it hung gracefully down her back like long strands of golden silk.

She hadn't worn too much makeup tonight—just enough eyeliner to give her large almond-shaped eyes a slightly smoky look, and a natural-coloured lip gloss to emphasise her new-found pout. She hadn't put foundation on for the first time in years and was amazed at how much prettier she looked as her exposed skin showed off her youthful glow. She looked fresh and natural. And happy.

It hadn't taken long to decide what to wear as she didn't have a huge collection of posh frocks. She obviously couldn't wear the new dress she'd worn to dinner on Saturday, so that really only left the old faithful little black dress, which covered all eventualities. It made her slender figure look sexy and the high heels on her black patent shoes made her taller than her usual five foot four.

She did a little twirl in front of the full-length mirror, stopping so that her back was facing the glass, and looked over her shoulder to study her rear view. She lifted the skirt of her dress to inspect her naked bottom, and sighed. The pale skin was unblemished—not even a tiny little red mark remained from last night's spankings. She was rather disappointed about that.

She looked at her watch. Ten minutes to go. She'd hardly seen Adam all day at the office—he'd been out at meetings for most of the day and the few times he'd been around, he'd been on the phone or with someone. He had politely nodded good morning to her as she'd brought in his coffee and had barely said goodbye as he'd rushed out at four o'clock for a meeting in Canary Wharf—she hadn't seen him or heard from him since.

At seven twenty-five, she put her coat on and stood by

the window to look out for the car. Mandy was working late so Rachel was alone with plenty of time to count the minutes and contemplate the night ahead. Where would he be taking her tonight? What was it he was planning to do to her on Friday night at Boundaries, and what would his house be like when he took her home afterwards? Would he have a dungeon in the cellar?

The sound of a car horn told her Rob, Adam's driver, was waiting and so she hurriedly grabbed her bag and made her way downstairs. He was holding the passenger door open for her and she smiled her thanks as she climbed into the car. She'd been hoping to see Adam waiting for her, but the car was empty.

"Where's Adam?" she asked, as Rob fastened his seatbelt then pulled away from the kerb.

"He'll be waiting for you when you arrive."

"Arrive where?"

He didn't reply, just kept his eyes on the road and left her alone with her memories of the journey home last night. Her face heated when she thought about the erotic spanking Rob had witnessed in the back and she was thankful for his discreet silence. She fixed her eyes on the passing lamp posts and settled back to enjoy the ride with nervous anticipation.

After a while, she noticed Rob wasn't heading towards central London as she had been expecting, but was driving towards Highgate. *Where are we going?* Finally he drove past Hampstead Heath and turned into Hampstead High Street. Were they going to a restaurant here? Hampstead Village was famous for being trendy and expensive. A restaurant here would undoubtedly be very good.

Rob turned into a narrow side road off the High Street and continued down to the bottom where he turned again into an even narrower, cobbled lane. The only light came from Victorian style lamp posts — apart from that, they seemed to be in the middle of nowhere. She swallowed nervously and wondered what the hell Adam was up to.

Rob pulled slowly up the lane then came to a stop by a row of Victorian terraced cottages. Without a word, he got out and opened the door for her.

"Where is this?" she whispered as she climbed out of the car and looked around.

Rob just tipped his hat and turned his head towards the shiny black door of the whitewashed cottage in front of them. "Mr Stone is waiting for you, Miss."

"Is this Adam's house?" she gasped. Of all the places she had imagined Adam to live, this cute cottage was definitely not one of them.

Rob smiled and nodded, letting her know in his usual discreet way that this was indeed Adam's house.

"Wow. Thanks, Rob." She walked up to the front door and rang the bell, excitement building inside her at the prospect of seeing Adam again, outside work. She heard footsteps approach, then the door opened, allowing warm, welcoming light and a delicious smell of home cooking to waft out. Adam smiled as he held the door for her to enter and took her coat once she was inside.

More books from
Katy Swann

Book three in the Boundaries series

*First she submitted, then she learnt to trust, but can
Rachel finally promise to obey?*

More books from
Katy Swann

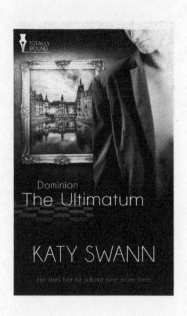

*Once a submissive, always a submissive, right? Maybe she
needs a little reminder.*

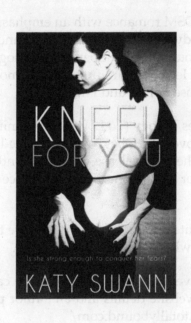

KNEEL FOR YOU

Is she strong enough to conquer her fears?

KATY SWANN

Should she agree to be spanked? Just the once? It would all be in the name of research, of course…

About the Author

Katy Swann

Katy Swann is in her forties and lives near London, UK with her husband, three children and two cats.

Katy writes BDSM romance with an emphasis on D/s. She finds the D/s dynamic the most exciting and erotic aspect of BDSM although a good spanking or flogging comes a close second. Her books are first and foremost love stories with a large dose of D/s and kinky sex.

The Boundaries Trilogy (To Love and Submit, To Love and Trust & To Love and Obey) was published in December 2013 and was her first release. She is currently working on a new series of standalone BDSM romance novels called Dominion.

Coffee, chocolate and cats are her favourite things and are often close by when she sits down to write.

Katy Swann loves to hear from readers. You can find contact information, website details and an author profile page at https://www.totallybound.com/

TOTALLY
BOUND

Home of Erotic Romance